More of EVERYTHING ACCORDING to ALEX

Kathryn Lamb

PICCADILLY PRESS • LONDON

For my family

Typeset from author's disc by Textype
in 10.5pt Palatino and 14pt Soupbone bold

Printed and bound in Great Britain by
WBC Book Manufacturers, Bridgend
for the publishers Piccadilly Press Ltd,
5 Castle Road, London NW1 8PR

A catalogue record for this book is available
from the British Library

ISBNs: 1 85340 680 5 (hardback)
         1 85340 675 9 (trade paperback)

10 9 8 7 6 5 4 3 2 1

Cover design by Judith Robertson

Tuesday August 15th

Bored. Nothing to do except write in this diary. Time for a brief recap on all the important people in my life who, I have to say, are doing NOTHING to alleviate my boredom! (No doubt they all have better things to do . . . SIGH.)

Friends

Abby: Best Friend

ABBY (WITH HER FABBY NEW HAIRSTYLE)

Age: 15
Fun to be with (except when she's in a mood!). We share our innermost thoughts and our outermost clothes, although we are different sizes (meaning that she has a fantastic figure and I DON'T). We also share similar tastes in BOYS, which can cause PROBLEMS (you can take sharing too far . . .). Abby is an only child and has a boyfriend called James.

Tracey (also known as Trez): Good Friend
Age: 15 years, 11 months and 29 days
(PARTY TIME! Although Tracey has decided to have a party in September because she's gone with her family on an exotic holiday in the Caribbean for most of August –

5

some people have all the luck!!!) She makes us all laugh – although someone should tell her you can take a joke TOO FAR (I didn't think I looked THAT funny in the bottle-green flares . . .). Tracey went out with a boy called Zak for two weeks, but they broke up after she told him his feet smelled like rotting Gorgonzola cheese. (You can have too much honesty in a relationship . . .)

Rowena (also known as Rowz – pronounced Rose): Sort of Friend
Age: 16
Très sportif, which I believe is French for mad on everything from hockey to bungee jumping, and built like a gladiator. She worries me. Finding a boyfriend called Edward seems to have had a calming influence on her (she doesn't challenge me to arm-wrestling competitions quite so frequently) but has done nothing to dampen her enthusiasm for SPORT.

Clare (also known as Clam because she doesn't say very much): Quiet Friend (Except when giggling . . .)
Age: 15 going on 12
Still has tendency to giggle helplessly during Biology lessons (and also during Geography, although no one is quite sure why). To everyone's surprise (because she never wears make-up and has super-protective parents who send her to bed at nine every night with a warm milky drink) she now has a BOYFRIEND called

Simon. But if anything, this has made the giggling WORSE. Clare works V. HARD and keeps her room scrupulously neat and tidy, and we are all very concerned about her.

Mark . . . (The name makes me melt . . . !)
Age: 16 (Older than me, which is *reeeally* exciting! When I am 16, he will be nearly 17!!!) BOYfriend. Or should I say boyFRIEND? Sometimes I think that he is just a friend. Sometimes I think that he is just a boy. Sometimes I think that life is hideously confusing. Mark is OK. That's all I'm prepared to say. For now.

MARK (SIGH!)

Family

Dad
Name: Hank (Embarrassing.)
Age: 146½
Dad is brilliant with computers but is very puzzled indeed by teenage daughters.

Mum
Name: Petunia Rose (Cringe.)
Age: 32 (This isn't true, but I get extra pocket money if I tell her she looks younger than she is. Flattery . . .)

Mum is always there when I need her (and also when I don't). Has tendency to fly into purple-faced, screaming rage if my room is not tidy. She and Dad should try to chill out more (and get out more, leaving the house to ME).

Siblings
Far too many of them, so having the house to myself is DIFFICULT.

Big Sissy
Age: 19
Also known as Daisy Henrietta. She's working at a local garden centre before going on to do a teacher-training course. She has a weird-looking librarian boyfriend called Diggory, who is quite nice really (he can't help looking like a giraffe and making a snorting noise through his nose when he laughs . . .). I admire my sister. She is BIG and BEAUTIFUL (although she would prefer it if I cut out the word BIG). We get on well (especially if I leave her perfume/lipstick/shoes, etc. alone . . .).

Recurring Nightmares (otherwise known as BROTHERS):

Daniel Nathaniel Fitt
Age: 13
Main characteristic: Spotty

Sebastian Jervase Fitt

Age: 11

Main characteristic: Snotty

These two (Spotty and Snotty) share a room, and they have pinned a notice on the door which reads BOY ZONE. I have to say that the day I see crowds of screaming girls surging into my brothers' room begging for their autographs (or worse), I will eat my hat. (But not the black felt one which I like and may one day dare to wear in public – at the moment I only wear it in the bathroom, with the door locked. OK, so I'm weird. I admit it. Having three younger brothers is enough to drive any girl to insanity, and back.)

Henry Algernon Fitt

Age: 8

Main characteristic: Annoying

All three brothers seem to think it is a great joke to burst into my room when I have friends round and pull stupid faces (or maybe those are their normal faces and they just can't help looking stupid . . .). In VERY small doses, and taken individually, my brothers have occasionally been bearable, even quite sweet (what am I saying?!!!!!). Daniel lent me a tape once, WITHOUT asking for anything in return! (Wow.)

Smallest Sibling of them All

Rosie Clementine

Age: Nearly 4 (Which means there will be a birthday party soon, and You Know Who will be expected to assist with Pass the Parcel, feeding time, and escorting guests to the loo after they have stuffed themselves with too many sausages, crisps, etc. FUN.)

My friends all think that Rosie is CUTE (these are the same poor, deluded friends who think that I am LUCKY to have so many brothers and sisters . . .). She *is* pretty, I suppose (which stands to reason, since she is related to ME . . .).

It seems a bit sad to cite the cat/hamsters, etc. as being 'important people' in my life. So I won't mention them.

Wednesday August 16th

I am in LURVE!!! Did I say that Mark was OK? Well, he's better than that. In fact, he's THE BEST. He was around at the time when a boy who shall remain nameless (Kevin) broke my heart. I never noticed Mark very much, although my friends said he fancied me like mad! And now that Kevin is a Thing of the Past, I am glad to say the feeling is mutual (I fancy Mark too). We have been going out together now for a WHOLE MONTH!!! We go out every day to walk the neighbour's dog whose name is Dogbert. Sometimes we walk the dog three or four times in one day! Dogbert has never had so much exercise, and I swear that his legs are getting shorter. (In fact, he is dog-tired, ha ha.) Mum makes me

DOGBERT

take my darling little sister Rosie with us quite often, but it doesn't matter since Mark thinks she is CUTE, and Dogbert likes her too. Just occasionally I wonder if Mark will think of inviting me to do something else apart from walk the dog. Have tried dropping heavy hints about films I would like to see, etc. No success yet. But I will wait for him, no matter how long it takes.

Thursday August 17th

'I have a nice surprise for you, Alex!' says Dad. (What is it? Has he decided to increase my allowance/install

THE DOG'S LEGS ARE GETTING SHORTER (FROM SO MANY WALKS)

some state-of-the-art hi-fi equipment in my room/move the rest of the family including himself and Mum to another house, not too far away, so that I have more room in this one for all my stuff, friends, parties, etc? NO. Noooooooooo . . .) The sad truth (the DEVASTATING truth!!!) is that he has booked a family holiday (aaargh!!!) at the Happy Hooray Holidays 'R' Us Fun Camp in a remote part of North Wales. (What has got into him? Is he going through a mid-life crisis? I have heard Mum say to a friend that he has been going through one for at least the last fifteen years – my entire life.) I consider phoning Abby or the Samaritans for help and advice but I am too embarrassed. Why couldn't Dad have chosen the South of France for a family holiday instead of some NAFF holiday camp in darkest Wales? I try one last desperate appeal to Dad's remaining sanity (if it exists):

'Er, that's great, Dad,' I say, forcing a ghastly grin. (The poor old chap looks so pleased at what he has done that I don't wish to be too hard on him.) 'But it would be really useful if we could go to France instead because I'm taking French for GCSE. I'm not doing Welsh. No one is.'

Friday August 18th

I am in my room packing to go to the Happy Hooray Holidays 'R' Us Fun Camp. Dad has been raving on incessantly about how lucky he was to book our holiday at the Fun Camp so late in the season. I have tried, without success, to explain to him that it is because no one else wants to go there.

'Mark's here, dear!' Mum calls to me up the stairs. She always puts on a silly, trilly and unsuitably skittish and girly tone of voice when informing me that Mark is at the door (EMBARRASSING).

Mark seems taken aback at the sight of my bulging suitcase (plenty of warm clothing, etc. and a number of dark, sombre outfits befitting the occasion).

'How long are you going for?'

'A week.'

'Oh. I'll . . . I'll . . . I'll, er, miss you.'

He tries to give me a kiss, but I have too much to say to him, so I move to one side and continue, 'I know. It's awful. I'll try to phone. And I'll write. But I don't even know if the post reaches where we're going. You'll just have to address your letters to the Happy Hooray Holidays 'R' Us Fun Camp, Wales, and hope for the best. There is a place name but it's unpronounceable and I'm not even going to try to spell it.'

Mark looks unhappy, so I make a brave attempt to

lighten up. 'Hey, we'll keep in touch somehow! OK? I just hate saying goodbye and you're making it really difficult.'

'I am?'

'Yes. Just don't

say another word. Let's remember this moment. But you'd better leave now. Promise you won't forget me.'

'Right. So you don't want to walk the dog today, then?'

'Pleeease, Mark! Don't make this harder than it already is.'

Reluctantly, Mark leaves, and I throw myself on my bed and weep bitter tears at the pain of parting. How can my parents tear me away like this when things are going so well between me and Mark? I am particularly incensed that Big Sissy does not have to come on this holiday because she is over eighteen. A pathetic excuse, if ever I heard one. And Mum and Dad let her get away with it!

Saturday August 19th

The journey to Wales is really BAD as Rosie is sick three times and I am squashed up close to my three brothers with no means of escape, which is a situation I usually go out of my way to avoid. Our vehicle is groaning under the weight of several tons of luggage, beach balls, tennis rackets, golf clubs and Dad's moth-collecting equipment. I have a horrible suspicion that trapping a few moths is as exciting as the nightlife gets.

The Fun Camp is everything I expected it to be, and worse. With a wild whoop of joy Dad seizes his golf clubs and rushes on to the crazy golf course while the

DAD IS IN HOLIDAY MOOD

rest of us settle into our chalet which is like being at home again, only a lot more cramped.

Sunday August 20th

Dad trapped two moths last night. Mum is busy doing all the washing by hand as the Happy Hooray Holidays 'R' Us launderette flooded last night and is temporarily out of action. Unfortunately the Happy Hooray payphone was vandalised the day before we arrived, but there is a man working on it at the moment so I should be able to phone Mark soon (parents too mean to give me my own mobile). My brothers have gone off to make nuisances of themselves at the pool, and I am left to take Rosie for her seventh go on the bouncy castle since we arrived. The weather is cool and overcast, but it is not actually raining.

Monday August 21st

It rained heavily all night and the bulb in Dad's special moth lamp exploded with a bang which woke us all up and brought several camp attendants running with excited cries to find out if someone had been shot.

10 a.m. – It is still raining, and we are all cooped up in our chalet. Dad suggests a drive, so we pile into the family vehicle again and set off. The bottles of sunscreen and economy cans of mosquito repellent which Mum thoughtfully brought with us seem unnecessary, although I wouldn't mind a super-economy can of sheep repellent since there are sheep EVERYWHERE. And not a lot else. Rosie is sick again.

ROSIE IS SICK AGAIN

1.30 p.m. – Back at camp. The man is still working on the payphone but he does not seem to be having much success. We all go to have lunch at the Happy Hooray Holidays 'R' Us Eaterie (which is quite a mouthful, ha ha). The food and the smell are uncannily reminiscent of the school canteen, and the only light relief is provided by the presence of a *reeeally* dishy boy (probably older than me) who works at the camp and is cleaning tables. When he comes to clear our table I try to pretend that I am not part of my family but just happen to be sitting with them (I wish I hadn't chosen a stupid Kids' Club Handi Havasnak box, decorated with cute jungle creatures. He must think I'm about twelve).

'Do you want your free Kute Toy, Alex?' asks Rosie. 'You got the thnake. I want the thnake. I only got the effalunt. I don't like effalunts. I want your thnake.'

'Shut up.'

'Alex, that's not very nice. Poor Rosie.'

Tuesday August 22nd

There are now two repair men looking at the payphone and scratching their heads, but it is still out of order. The weather has brightened up and Dad has gone back to have another round on the crazy golf course. So far everyone has beaten him, and he is becoming increasingly stressed by the situation, blaming his clubs and the way the course is laid out.

I wander off to send my third postcard to Mark (a panoramic view of beautiful Llandafdaffy Bay which no one round here seems to know how to get to, and it isn't on the map so we haven't been there). There doesn't seem to be another collection from the postbox until Thursday (it doesn't say which Thursday . . . Thursday December 17th in the year 2020?) so I am not sure when or if Mark will get his postcards. Just in case he does ever receive them, I have told him how much I am missing him. I have also added a 'P.S. I miss you' and a 'P.P.S. I miss you loads'. I think he should get the message. I guess I am feeling guilty about fancying someone else.

Wednesday August 23rd

I spend a lot of time hanging out in the Happy Hooray Eaterie, making a can of Coke and a Happisnak last as long as possible so that I can watch the gorgeous boy who clears the tables (without being too obvious). Luckily there is a large mirror on the wall near-by so I can check my hair and make-up at regular intervals (again, without being too obvious). I find myself spending the money I was keeping for the phone on crisps and packets of biscuits (not because I am hungry but because the more rubbish I have on my table the more likely HE is to come and clear it!).

My family arrives at the eaterie for lunch and they show signs of wanting to sit with me. So I get up and move to another table. I explain that I want them to be comfortable and have more leg room so it might be better if I went and sat somewhere else. They look slightly taken aback, but wisely they decide not to argue with me. I choose a table with plenty of rubbish. HE comes over with a tray and starts clearing MY table. I feel myself going hot all over. My brothers are nudging each other, sniggering and pointing. (*How* do they know?) Mum and Dad, who can be quite sensible at times, tell my brothers to behave or they won't have their KiddiKrunchburgers with Megachips. This is enough to shut them up.

HE CLEARS MY TABLE !!!

'What's your name?' (Oh my god, HE is talking to ME!!!)

'Er . . . er . . . it's . . .' (Damn! I've forgotten!!!)

'Hang on a minute! It'll come back to me. Alex! Yes, it's Alex! That's my name. Phew! What's yours?'

'Jack.'

'Hi, Jack.' (Oh god. Did I just say 'hijack'? He must get that all the time . . .)

'Hi, Alex. Look, I'm a bit busy at the moment but I've got the morning off tomorrow. I'll show you round the camp if you like.'

'Oh, wow! I mean, yeah. That'd be great. I mean cool. Fine. OK.'

'Meet you here about ten?'

'Sure.'

Thursday August 24th

Dad has been banned from the crazy golf course as a result of seriously losing his cool with the Wacky Mini-Watermill Trick Shot after missing it completely for the tenth time in succession. He hit the synthetic turf such a wallop with his golf club that it made a small hole. Several onlookers went and told on him, and so he has been banned.

I feel sorry for Dad. First the moths. Now this. But Dad has always refused to accept total defeat, and so he has decided that today he is going to find Llandafdaffy Bay, home of the very rare Llandafdaffy

LLANDAFDAFFY DUCK

duck. He wants to take all of us with him but I remind him that I really do want everyone to be comfortable, and they would all have more leg room if I was not in the car. This time Dad looks set to argue with me, but Mum takes him by the arm and shakes her head. The result is that I am allowed to stay behind!

Dad is keen to get off to an early start and he has my full support in this. I help to get the whole family and their buckets and spades loaded into the car, and wave a fond farewell as they set off in the direction of Llandafdaffy Bay (they are all relying on Mum's instinctive sense of direction, so their day is certainly doomed).

Now I'm in a happy hooray holiday mood! I quickly change out of my dull, everyday clothes (which I put on to reassure the rest of the family of my quiet and sensible nature) and pull on my glittery white top with the thin straps and a black micro-skirt with a little slit up one side (Is this a bit OTT? I dither horribly, then change into a slightly

A LITTLE OVER THE TOP..?
(AND EVEN LESS OVER THE BOTTOM!)

longer skirt with a slit up the back). I have three minutes to apply make-up and do my hair.

I arrive at the Happy Hooray Eaterie in a breathless and hyperactive frame of mind, and wonder if Jack will mind if I have several goes on the bouncy castle in order to get the excess energy out of my system (it is unusual for me to feel like this at ten in the morning!). Is he ever going to turn up? I search anxiously – but there is no sign. Despair!!! Then someone taps me on the shoulder and I leap into the air as if I am already on the bouncy castle.

'Sorry – I didn't mean to make you jump. Want to go for a wander?'

Jack looks different, and then I realise that he no longer has on the little red apron that he wears for work. He is even better looking without it!

We discover that we have loads in common – embarrassing families (he has *eight* brothers and sisters!!!) and a strong dislike of school. He is working at the camp as a holiday job, but he has to go back to school to retake several exams, and his parents want him to stay on at school and take MORE EXAMS! We sympathise with each other. We have a common understanding of the problems of parental pressure and the difficulty of getting away from the ever-present hordes of brothers and sisters.

I show him our chalet. Then he shows me round the back of the chalet and kisses me before I really know

what is happening. His arms are all around me and he is obviously thinking in terms of a really long, hot snog. But I don't know. It is all a bit sudden. I need time to think. I pull away.

'Oh. I thought you wanted me to kiss you.'

'Er . . . yes. But. Can I get back to you on this one? We could meet up later . . . or something?'

Jack shrugs and wanders away. 'I'll see you around,' he calls over his shoulder.

'I'll give you my address!' I call back. 'We could write to each other!'

Friday August 25th

My legs are black and blue from having kicked myself all last night. What kind of an IDIOT am I??! A mega-droolworthy, drop-dead gorgeous boy tries to kiss me, and what do I do? I PUSH HIM AWAY!!! I try to console myself with the thought that he smelled a bit strange – a curious mixture of chips, cheeseburgers and Stynx 2000 (*the* hot smell for the new millennium!). Mark smells a lot nicer . . .

I am now besieged by pangs of guilt about what I have done and how hurt Mark would be if he knew. Which he doesn't.

There are now three men trying to mend the payphone, and two of them are in a heated argument as I walk by, while the third one is hitting the phone with a large spanner. I wish I could call Mark – just to say hello (nothing more) and hear his voice . . .

Dad is in a foul mood after failing to find Llandafdaffy Bay. The family arrived back late last night after spending nearly the whole day in the car, driving in ever-decreasing circles, rather like the Llandafdaffy duck, which is renowned for swimming in circles. Dad blames Mum (for everything) and Mum blames Dad for wanting to go in the first place, and they both blame the man who gave them directions. The same man told them that his brother-in-law kept two breeding pairs of Llandafdaffy ducks but he fed them on laver bread and they all died. Rosie

I WANT TO GO HOME...

DEAD LLANDAFDAFFY DUCK

woke up twice in the night, crying about the dead ducks.

I want to go home.

Saturday August 26th

The payphone is mended! Unfortunately I have spent the last of my phone money on a little souvenir plaster model of a duck for Rosie (I am so WONDERFUL), and Mum and Dad are too generally bad-tempered and preoccupied with packing to give me any more.

I have felt too embarrassed to go near the Happy Hooray Eaterie since my ill-fated meeting with Jack on Thursday. But I would like to see him one last time before we leave – and I am also exceeeeedingly hungry.

I have planned what I am going to say to him: I really like you, Jack. But it could never work. You see – there's someone back home . . .

As I enter the Happy Hooray Eaterie I see Jack over at a table where a girl is sitting, wearing a skirt so incredibly

JACK THE RAT

short it could more accurately be described as a belt. Jack hasn't noticed me and, as I pass by, I hear him ask the girl if she would like him to show her round the camp later. The RAT!!!

Turning my back on Jack (in every sense) I order a double portion of Megachips and a Brunchburger, and indulge in some serious comfort eating. I feel sick on the journey home. In the end, Rosie and I are both sick.

Of course, it was not just the junk food which made me sick. It was the thought of Jack! How could he have behaved the way he did? My stressed brain comes up with a number of possible reasons:

1) In reality, he is very shy, and has to force himself to pluck up the courage to talk to girls. He didn't really want to talk to the girl in the very short skirt. It was a sort of personal challenge that he set himself.
2) He is such a sweet person that he cannot help being friendly.
3) He was so devastated by my rejection of him that he had to throw himself at the nearest girl. If I had spoken to him and told him that I really liked him, he might have broken down and apologised to me for his behaviour with the other girl, possibly even going down on bended knee to tell me of his undying love . . .
4) On further consideration, I think he is probably a RAT.

I pass the rest of the journey with my eyes closed, trying not to think.

'Thanks, Dad,' I say when we eventually reach home. 'It's been great.' Dad looks unconvinced.

Sunday August 27th

I have been feeling too ill and tired to see or even talk to any of my friends. But now Mark is at the door, and Mum is her old skittish and girlish self again (I wish she wasn't). I suppose I must face Mark sooner or later. (I have to question how strong my feelings for him really are, if I could so easily fall for someone else. I keep thinking about Jack, even if he is a RAT.)

'Hi, Alex! It's good to see you. Want to walk the dog?'

'You didn't write to me. Not once. I wrote to you.'

'I know. Thanks. I liked the postcards. I was going to write. But I couldn't remember the address.'

'HAH!!!'

'What's that supposed to mean?'

'It means "HAH!!!" I suppose you forgot ME, as well??!!?'

'Er . . . no.'

'There's someone else, isn't there?'

'No, Alex, there's no one else. What's got into you? You're behaving really strangely.'

I know I am. I suppose I am trying to shift my own guilty feelings on to Mark's shoulders. I realise how unfair this is. 'Look, Mark, I'm sorry. I'm just not feeling very well. I'll catch up with you later, if that's OK.'

As soon as Mark has gone, I phone Abby for help and advice. They say that confession is good for the soul, so I tell her EVERYTHING. (Dad walks past while I am on the phone and I have to switch from describing my passionate embrace with Jack to saying in a loud voice: 'And the scenery was extremely beautiful.')

'You were looking at the scenery?' says Abby in a puzzled voice.

'It's OK. Dad's gone. Oh, Abby – what am I going to do? I feel awful.'

'Well, if you don't tell Mark, he'll never know.'

I see the logic of Abby's advice, and feel better.

'On the other hand,' continues Abby, 'if you don't tell him what you have done, it will always be on your conscience and every time Mark kisses you, you will remember how you have betrayed him, and betrayed your love, and . . .'

'Yes, yes – OK! Thanks. So you think I ought to tell him?'

'It is entirely a matter for your own conscience. But I think you ought to tell him.'

Abby has convinced me. I *have* to tell Mark. I must be honest with him, even if he hates me for it. But I hope he won't. Perhaps he will admire me for my honesty.

I decide to sleep on it.

Monday August 28th

I wake up knowing that I am RIGHT to be HONEST. With a great surge of personal integrity I march straight round to Mark's house and ask his mum to leave us alone for a moment as I have something important to say to her son. Looking slightly taken aback she retreats to the kitchen and closes the door behind her.

Mark does not seem to be fully awake yet. He is sitting in front of the TV in his T-shirt and shorts, eating a huge bowl of Krumblekrunch (it's the Krunchiest Krumble! Or the Krumbliest Krunch). His hair is tousled (SEXEEE!!!). I am momentarily thrown off tack and forget why I am there. Then I remember.

JUST GOT OUT OF BED EYES

ER – WHAT AM I DOING HERE?

I decide to come straight out with it.

'Mark, there's something I have to tell you. When I was in Wales I kissed a boy called Jack behind the chalet.'

'Behind the what?'

'The chalet. We stayed in a chalet. The important thing is that I kissed a boy.'

'Called Jack?'

'Yes.'

'Why?'

'I don't know WHY! I'm SORRY. OK?'

'You don't sound it.'

'Well, I am. This is difficult for me.'

Mark sighs, and puts down his bowl of Krumblekrunch. He seems to have lost his appetite. I get the distinct impression that he does not admire me for my honesty.

'So. Are you going to see him again?'

'I think it's unlikely.'

'But you'd like to?'

'I, er . . . no. I mean . . . no. He's a rat.'

'You kissed a rat. Didn't you think about me at all?'

'Yes! I did! All the time!'

'Except when you were kissing Jack.'

'Look – can we just drop the subject? I've said I'm sorry.'

Mark hangs his head in his hands. Is he crying? Oh, god – what have I done?

Suddenly he leaps up and mutters something about having to go into town to get some things for school. 'So, I'll see you around,' he says, without really looking at me. I think I get the picture. He is shutting me out. I expect I have wounded the male ego. (I have heard Mum talk about this phenomenon with reference to Dad and certain remarks which were made about his thinning hair and thickening waistline.)

Mark's mum pokes her head out from behind the kitchen door and says, 'Can I come out now?' in a silly voice which is strangely reminiscent of the silly voice which my own mum puts on whenever Mark and I are together.

Monday September 4th

A whole week has gone by and I have hardly seen Mark at all. When I passed him the other day (Saturday, I think), he was incredibly cool towards me. (I mean he was distant and stand-offish – I don't mean he was behaving like a real cool dude! Unfortunately.) We haven't taken the dog for a single walk and when I last saw Dogbert, he looked almost as miserable as Mark. And that's MISERABLE.

THE DOG IS MISERABLE

I am *almost* looking forward to going back to St Rhubarb's

tomorrow. I am certainly looking forward to seeing my friends.

Tuesday September 5th

By mid-morning I have already had ENOUGH of listening to Tracey rave on about her wonderful exotic Caribbean holiday and her wonderful exotic Caribbean boyfriend, whose name is Dean and who actually proposed marriage to her at a special beach party which her parents laid on to celebrate her sixteenth birthday. She has a wonderful exotic engagement ring to prove it. She says that they are planning a long engagement, but they are sending faxes and e-mails to each other every day in the meantime.

TRACEY TELLS US ABOUT DEAN (AND
THEN SHE TELLS US AGAIN...AND AGAIN...)

'So how was your holiday, Alex?' asks Tracey.

'Ah. Er . . . great. We went to Wales. Beautiful scenery. Lots of sheep. I met someone called Jack.'

'Oh, wow! Tell us! Go on! Does Mark know?'

'Er, yes. He's not cool about it.'

'You did the right thing, Alex. Telling him.'

'Yes, Abby. Thanks.'

'It's OK.'

'So tell us about Jack!'

'Er . . .'

Fortunately the bell rings for the next lesson, and I am spared the necessity of trying to explain what happened behind the chalet (not much). I am torn between the desire to make my holiday sound vaguely interesting and the sneaking suspicion that anything I say will get back to Mark and cause even more hurt. I don't want to hurt him. I really like him! But he is avoiding me, and when I caught his eye this morning he looked away quickly. He has HURT written all over him, and obviously intends to make me feel BAD.

MARK HAS HURT WRITTEN ALL OVER HIM

James and Gary keep pestering me with

stupid questions, such as: 'What have you done to Mark, Alex?' 'Have you hurt his feelings?' 'Don't you want to kiss him?' 'Is JACK better at kissing than he is? Can't he handle it?' They keep sniggering in a way that is horribly reminiscent of my own brothers' behaviour. I tell them to shut up, and Abby tells them to shut up (although I have my suspicions that she has been talking to James, and that is how the embarrassing gossip and rumours have started). I am bright red in the face and my ears are burning by the time I get to the next lesson, which is Art.

Art is my best subject and I am taking it for GCSE. Mark is also taking an Art GCSE, not because he is good at Art (I have to say he isn't) but because we wanted to take the same subjects as each other in order to spend as much time together as possible. Mark had to argue very hard indeed to be allowed to take Art for GCSE. The Art teacher tried hard to put him off (she couldn't stand looking at his horrible daubs any longer). We are all very suspicious that Mark's decision to take Art for GCSE was the reason she left.

The new Art teacher is called Miss Ziggle. She is American, young and VERY pretty, and positively radiates creative energy. The boys are all instantly mesmerised, and I suspect that there will be a few more who have shown no previous interest in Art who will now be clamouring to be allowed to take it for GCSE.

MISS ZIGGLE

Wednesday September 6th

The boys in our year (Year Eleven) seem moody and distracted until the bell rings for the next Art lesson. Suddenly there is a wild stampede and they are all in the Art room, sitting to attention, awaiting the arrival of their goddess. The girls filter in at a more leisurely (and sane) pace, and we all look suitably bored and fed up at the boys' moronic behaviour.

There is nearly a nasty accident as six or more boys all rush to the door at once to hold it open for Miss Ziggle.

'Pleeease! Boys! Relax! We must all be relaxed in order that our creative energy can flow. So, everyone, take deeeeeep breaths. In. And out.'

The sound of the boys' heavy breathing is certainly audible. I ask Miss Ziggle if I can open a window since I feel in need of some fresh air. It would seem that all the boys have discovered Stynx 2000, and the smell is overwhelming. They have all obviously had baths in it, in order to impress the Ziggle with the Wiggle (as the wittier girls, such as Abby, Tracey and myself, have named her).

Miss Ziggle tells us that she will be awarding a special prize at the end of term for the pupil producing the most consistently high standard of work. This is to be part of a special awards ceremony for Year Eleven which the school has decided to introduce as an incentive towards better exam results. Miss Ziggle tells us that the prizes will include tokens to spend in a nearby record store, and that they will be presented by a mystery 'celebrity' guest speaker. There is an excited babble of voices trying to guess who this will be. Most of the boys are hoping it will be Synthia Snoberts, dazzling star of many a successful film. (What planet do the boys live on? Do they really imagine a top Hollywood actress is going to come to St Rhubarb's

Comprehensive?) The girls are more realistic, so we are all hoping that the mystery celebrity will turn out to be delicious Dermot O'Flaherty, lead singer with the all-time mega successful boy group Dreamz. (Or it might be his younger brother, Matty O'Flaherty. Or, if we are *really* lucky, it might be dishy Ronan O'Hoolahan, who plays football *and* sings!)

DISHY RONAN O'HOOLAHAN (HE PLAYS FOOTBALL *AND* SINGS!)

Thursday September 7th

Clare follows me around when we get to school this morning. She keeps looking at me strangely, and it is obvious that she wants to ask me something.

'What IS it, Clare?'

'Er, I hope you don't mind me asking, Alex – but is it true what I've heard? That you are going to stay on a sheep farm in Wales at half-term with a boy called Jack, and that you kissed him solidly for half an hour almost without taking a breath in the middle of a field with a bull in it, and Jack wrestled with the bull and saved your life, and Mark cried for an hour when you told him you didn't love him any more, and threatened to knock Jack's teeth out, and . . .'

'NOOOOOO!!!'

Everyone in the room turns to stare at me, and then they start whispering. I CAN'T STAND IT. Let me out of here!

Fortunately, Tracey has brought in her holiday photos, which provide a distraction, so that people forget about me, Mark and Jack the Rat for a while. There are about one hundred and forty-four photographs and they are all, without exception, of the wonderful exotic Caribbean boyfriend, Dean. (I am a little disappointed by the name. Dean is a nice name but somehow not as exotic as I was expecting.)

'And this one's of Dean when he got out of the pool too quickly and his trunks came off!'

This photo instantly draws quite a large crowd of interested girls, and Clare gets the giggles.

I heave a deep sigh and move away. Abby comes to join me. 'Gets boring, doesn't it?' she sighs.

'Yes. Tracey's changed.'

'Yes, I think she has, too. She's not as funny as she used to be.'

'Yes. And a lot more boring.'

'I know what you mean. This year's going to be boring. Too much work.'

'How's things between you and James?'

'OK, I suppose. But he can be pretty boring.'

'Mark's boring, too.'

'Have you made it up with him?'

'No. He's still in a mood with me.'

'Boys are REALLY boring when they're in a mood.'

'Tell me about it.'

← green

ROB (SIGH..YEARN..)

There is a new boy in our year called Rob. He has short green (yes, green!) hair (like Astroturf!) and wonderful eyes with long lashes and a humorous look. He gives us both a little smile as he wanders by in a relaxed and unhurried manner.

Abby and I both sort of melt all over the table on which we are sitting.

'He's not boring.'

'No. He's cool.'

Friday September 8th

Tracey hands out invitations to her sixteenth birthday party for all her friends. It is going to be held at her

39

house and there will be a disco. Her mum and dad have said that all the boys have got to leave at midnight, but some of the girls can sleep over. Rowena is in serious training at the moment as she wants to win a sports scholarship, and she asks Tracey if it is OK if she brings her weights and cycling machine with her. Tracey looks slightly surprised but says it is no problem. She also tells us that Dean has promised to send a special fax at a certain time on the night of her party, and we have all got to gather around the fax machine when it arrives.

'Perhaps he's going to send a photocopy of his bottom!' shouts a boy, who shall not be named. (His name is Gary, and he's quite funny. Tracey does not think so.)

Clare is once again convulsed with uncontrollable giggles, and I am close to strangling her.

The next lesson is English and there is another new teacher. Her name is Mrs Jolly, but she isn't. At least, perhaps she is sometimes – when she's
with Mr Jolly, for
instance – but the sight
of the eager, upturned
faces of Year Eleven,
all brimful with enthu-
siasm for the coming

MRS JOLLY (NOT VERY)

year, does not seem to have gladdened her heart. (Please note the use of HEAVY IRONY – English is another of my better subjects.)

Mrs Jolly is not as pretty as Miss Ziggle, and is in the early stages of pregnancy (so it is rumoured). Her face has taken on a greenish hue and pained expression, which may have something to do with the overwhelming smell of Stynx 2000. The boys are obviously still washing in it.

'Are you all right, Miss?' asks a boy called Freddy, who has a kind heart.

'She's Mrs, you idiot!' hisses Gary. 'She's pregnant, so she's Mrs!'

'Not necessarily,' says someone.

This is all too much for Mrs Jolly, who has to make a sudden exit from the room. We hear her gagging in the corridor. When she returns she has wrapped her scarf across her mouth and nose. This makes it difficult to hear what she is saying, but at least she makes it through the rest of the lesson without throwing up.

Monday September 11th

The weekend break seems to have done Mrs Jolly some good, and she has dispensed with the scarf, although she insists that all windows are left wide open. It is a breezy day, and loose papers keep flying around the room.

Mrs Jolly tells us that there is to be a special prize for

poetry. It will be called the Jolly Poetry Award, and the winner will receive a small trophy, a book token and have their prize-winning poem published in the school magazine. This sounds like a punishment to most of us, apart from Clare. Clare has been heavily into poetry ever since her boyfriend wrote her a love poem, which was later confiscated by her parents because it didn't scan (at least, that was the excuse they gave at the time).

An extra strong gust of wind blows Mrs Jolly's papers all round the room, and the rest of the lesson is spent retrieving them, putting them back in order, and handing them out.

I love school (IRONY).

Tuesday September 12th

Back in the Art room. The air is thick with teenage hormones, known as pheromones (and I hasten to add that they are not MY hormones, which have better things to do with themselves than fly round the Art room) and the rich and strange scent of Stynx 2000. I am not sure whether I like the smell, or not. I think . . . not.

Miss Ziggle unfolds a large poster of a sculpture of two people intertwined in a passionate embrace. She holds it up to the class.

'I want you to look at this,' she says. (No problem there – the boys are transfixed.)

'This is a famous sculpture by an artist called Rodin. It is called *The Kiss*.' (It certainly lives up to its name! The two seated figures in the sculpture have obviously got kissing down to a fine art . . .) 'I intend to use it as a starting point for your first assignment. I do not wish you to copy it, but I would like you to go home and draw your own interpretation of *The Kiss*. I will give you a week to do it. You may draw on your own experiences, if you like.'

This last remark provokes a little outburst of nervous laughter, and a few salacious sniggers from the back of the class. (Fortunately, Clare does not do Art, as we would have to carry her out, giggling.)

I think about Jack kissing me behind the chalet. Then I decide that I would rather forget about this, not *draw* it.

I notice Mark staring at me with a strangely resentful expression on his face. His determination to be utterly miserable is beginning to get on my nerves. Then I feel guilty for reacting like this. I didn't mean to hurt him. So I give him a friendly little wave. He pulls a face. (I am not sure what the face he is pulling is meant to convey, but it makes him look a bit like a duck, possibly a Llandafdaffy duck. Why doesn't he talk to me? I am not a mind-reader.)

At the end of the lesson Rob gives me a little half smile, and I have to admit that my heart skips a beat and now quite a number of my hormones perform handsprings all round the room. (Mark is being such a misery that I have decided that I should stop feeling guilty. I cannot put my entire life on hold because he is unable to deal with his own perfectly natural feelings of insane jealousy.)

MY HORMONES PERFORM HANDSPRINGS
ROUND THE ROOM...

Wednesday September 13th

Clare has joined library club, netball club, French club, drama club, the poetry and debating societies, needlework club (yes!) and Wednesday club. (No one knows what goes on at Wednesday club except that it takes place on Wednesday. Except once when it was postponed to Thursday.)

My friends and I think it is a naff thing to do to join all these clubs, and we tease Clare gently about it. But we are all startled into silence when Clare walks past,

CLARE WALKS PAST WITH <u>THE</u> MOST
GEORGEOUS BOY...

deep in conversation with *the* most GORGEOUS boy.

'Who was that?' we ask her at lunch. (We always meet in the canteen to exchange gossip, magazines, etc.)

'That's Ben,' she replies. 'He's just joined the Sixth Form. We met at French club, and he's asked me out.'

'But . . . what about Simon?' (This is Clare's boyfriend.)

'Simon and I sort of grew apart. I told him it was over. He was really upset. But Ben and I have loads in common, and it's fun going to French club together. That new boy, Rob – he goes to French club too.'

The rest of us are left wondering how someone like Clare manages to lead such an exciting love life. (Not that any of us is jealous, of course. Of course NOT.)

I nearly collide with Abby later in the day as I slink into the room where you go to join French club.

'Oh! Are you joining French club too?'

'Er . . . yes. I thought it might help. With the exam, I mean.'

'Me too. Yes. The French exam. I'm just so desperate to pass . . .'

'No, Alex. You're just desperate. Like me. Admit it.'

'OK, I admit it. Although we shouldn't be desperate. And you've already got a boyfriend.'

'Yeeees. I know. I just don't see myself stuck with James for the rest of my life.'

(I imagine Abby and James, both in their thirties or forties, hobbling into the sunset together. It is a bizarre and scary thought.)

'I just think James and I need to give each other space,' Abby continues. 'I told him I needed space.'

'What did he say?'

'Nothing. He just moved to another table and stared at me from across the room.'

'Boys are a problem.'

'They certainly are.'

Saturday September 16th

My weekends are so boring at the moment that I am reduced to sitting down to do my homework. I am under mounting pressure from the school, parents, even Big Sissy (who has a sadistic streak in her nature) to WORK HARD. I am beginning to feel like a zombie: **I MUST DO MORE WORK** . . . At least it is only a week until Tracey's party, which should provide some light relief, as long as she does not intend to hold a wake for absent Dean (I can imagine us all sitting in silence holding candles and remembering the ONE who is so far away . . .).

I spread out my Art folder on the dining-room table, which is the only table in the house large enough to take it (Art is a BIG subject). I feel uninspired. Then an image of Rob floats into my mind and with a sudden, unexpected burst of creative energy I draw two people in a passionate embrace. It looks obscene. Hastily checking that no other members of the family are around, I try to rub out bits of it (I won't tell you which bits, in case your younger brother or sister has got hold of this diary and is reading it). This makes it look even worse, as if I'm trying to conceal something *really* awful.

I am uncomfortably aware that there are now other people in the room, looking over my shoulder (I *wish* they wouldn't do this!!!).

'That's nice, dear!' says Mum, trying unconvincingly to be broadminded.

'Surely they shouldn't be encouraged to produce things like this!' exclaims Dad. 'I shall write to the school.' (Oh no. Dad has written so many letters to the school over the years that they must have an entire file or filing cabinet devoted to his correspondence.)

'The noses are all wrong,' observes Big Sissy, helpfully. (Noses are always a problem, whether you're drawing a kiss or actually kissing.)

BIG PEOPLE KISSING –
RUDE!

THE FAMILY LOOK OVER MY SHOULDER
(I WISH THEY WOULDN'T !)

'Why worry?' says Big Sissy's boyfriend, Diggory. 'Picasso drew some very strange noses and got away with it!'

'Big people kissing,' says Rosie. 'Rude.' This just about sums it up, and with an exclamation of extreme irritation I screw up my drawing into a ball and hurl it into a far corner.

'I think we'd better leave Alex now,' says Mum quietly, and the family makes a tactful withdrawal from the dining-room, although Dad is still muttering under his breath about declining standards and teachers setting a poor example.

A few minutes later my brothers burst into the room, find the screwed-up drawing and make off with it, sniggering horribly. How depressing. They're

Philistines, incapable of distinguishing between true art and . . . well, the sort of stuff they look at under the bedclothes at night. (Mum would have a fit if she knew!)

Sunday September 17th

Back to the drawing board. This time I decide to play it safe and I draw two people (fully clothed) kissing (the noses are *still* not right) and holding hands (aah!). No other body parts are touching.

Abby comes round to ask for my help with the Art homework. She has drawn herself and James kissing (they are also fully clothed, and each of them is standing

UNFORTUNATE ← INCIDENT INVOLVING CAT AND CAN OF COKE

← CRISIS OF CONFIDENCE CAUSED ME TO CHEW PAPER

MY DRAWING OF 'THE KISS.' (AREN'T THEY A DREEEAMY COUPLE? SHAME ABOUT THE NOSES).

on one leg, kicking up their other leg behind them. The pose looks distinctly precarious, and everything in the drawing is on a slant, so they are obviously about to fall over).

'I can't get the noses right,' says Abby.

'The noses are OK,' I reply. 'But I'm not sure about the legs. No, you've definitely caught the essence of James's nose. Large. Prominent.'

'James's nose is NOT large! James has a lovely nose. There's nothing prominent about it.'

'It's beautifully drawn. You are clever!'

Abby narrows her eyes and gives me a look. I don't want her to go into one of her moods. I *hate* it when she sulks!

'You're right, though,' she says. 'James *does* have a big nose. It gets in the way . . .'

That does it. We both collapse in fits of helpless mirth, and the Art homework is abandoned in favour of going up to my room to listen to music and to discuss James's nose in more detail. I read my horoscope (Gemini) in *YEZZ!* magazine. According to Mystic Marge, Mercury is aligned with Mars and the moon is in the seventh house of Venus, and it is therefore more than likely that I will meet a tall, dark and handsome stranger, who will sweep me off my feet. (I cannot help hoping that this tall, dark and handsome stranger MIGHT have green hair . . .)

Monday September 18th

On the way home from school I meet the owner of the dog which Mark and I used to walk. She has the dog with her. He has put on a lot of weight, and looks depressed.

'Dogbert's really missing his walks!' she says. 'I'm having a lot of trouble with my legs, and I can't really take him out as much as I should . . . I was hoping that you and young Mark might take him again – in return for a small reward, of course. He did so enjoy his walks with you . . .'

She looks down at Dogbert and shakes her head sadly. Dogbert stares at me forlornly and a little resentfully, in a way which strongly reminds me of the way Mark has been looking at me recently (I can't stand it!).

DOGBERT WORKS OUT!
(ONE OF MY BIZARRE THOUGHTS...)

'Don't worry,' I tell Dogbert's owner. 'I'll take him. Mark's probably busy at the moment. But I'll take him for a walk. If you want him to get some *real* exercise,' I add, 'I could put you in touch with a girl from my school called Rowena. She'd take him for a run!' (I imagine Rowena putting Dogbert through his paces on the cycling machine. It is a bizarre thought . . .)

While Dogbert and I are on our walk, we turn the corner and nearly collide with Mark coming in the opposite direction. Dogbert is overjoyed to see him, and nearly turns himself inside out, jumping up and trying to lick Mark's face. I feel no desire to behave like this.

Mark does not look overjoyed to see me, either. 'I see you're taking the dog for a walk,' he says in an accusatory tone of voice, as if I am committing some kind of major crime. 'WITHOUT ME.'

'The dog needed exercise.'

'Sure. So you'll go for a walk with the dog. But not with me.'

I do not believe it. I DO NOT BELIEVE IT. Mark is jealous of THE DOG! Are there *no* limits to his insane jealousy??!

'You're pathetic!' I snap. 'Come on, Dogbert. We're off!'

Tuesday September 19th

I feel bad about biting Mark's head off (metaphorically speaking), but Abby tells me I was right to be angry.

'It's time Mark grew up and learned to be more in control of his feelings,' she tells me. 'You deserve someone with a more mature attitude to life.'

'Good morning, girls!' Mr Chubb the Chemistry

GOOD MORNING, GIRLS!

MATURE

MATURE HAIR

MATURE

MATURE CLOTHES

MR CHUBB (MATURE)

MATURE SHAPE

ABBY TELLS ME I DESERVE SOMEONE MATURE ...

teacher greets us as we walk along the corridor.

'You mean, like Mr Chubb?' I ask, as soon as he is safely out of earshot.

'No, you idiot! I said *mature*, not *old*. They're two different things. Anyway, Mr Chubb's married.'

I pause to consider Mr Chubb in a state of marital bliss with Mrs Chubb and all the little Chubbs. It is almost as bizarre a thought as Dogbert on a bicycle.

'Do you think Rob's mature?' I ask.

'How should I know? You fancy him, don't you?'

'That's not a mature question.'

'No, but it's true, isn't it? You DO fancy him! What if I fancy him too?'

'What if . . . ?'

Thankfully, the bell rings, and it is time for Art. Everyone has brought in their drawings of people kissing. (One person – Gary – who had left his homework until the last minute, persuaded two of his friends to model a passionate embrace for him to draw. In fact, they didn't need much persuading . . . The result was that the two friends got into deep trouble for snogging in school, and all three were given detention.)

Miss Ziggle likes my drawing. (Gary hisses at me: 'Is that you and JACK?' I give him a look that could kill at thirty paces – except that Gary is too thick-skinned.) 'But I'm not sure about the noses,' says Miss Ziggle. (Thanks.) She draws me two wonderful noses, down to the last detail, such as the hint of a few hairs in each nostril and the vague suspicion of a bogey (she obviously belongs to the School of Sickening Realism). She shows me how two noses meet without bumping or getting in the way (Miss Ziggle must be brilliant at kissing!).

She is not sure about Mark's drawing (no one is). He has drawn only one person (at least, I think it's a person. It might be a tree).

'Where's the other person, Mark?'

'They've gone away.'

'Oh.'

'It's meant to be sad. You said we could draw on our own experiences.'

'Right. I see. OK. That's fine, Mark. I just don't think Rodin's *The Kiss* would have had the same impact if there had only been one person.'

She moves on to look at Rob's drawing, and her jaw sags slightly. The drawing is brilliant. It also leaves NOTHING to the imagination. All parts of the human anatomy (male and female) are there, in graphic detail. (I suspect that it is *too* realistic, even by Miss Ziggle's standards . . .)

'We could use that in Biology!' says a Great Wit (Gary).

Miss Ziggle seems at a loss for words. 'Er,' she says. 'Your drawing is technically brilliant, Rob.'

WHAT A COP-OUT!!!

ROB'S INTERPRETATION OF
'THE KISS'

Note: I am envious of Rob's artistic talent – it used to be ME who was The Best At Art – ahem, this is not a time for false modesty – but any feelings of envy I may have are cancelled out when I look at Rob's dreeeamy eyes and smoooochy mouth . . .

Wednesday September 20th

Several members of the Year Eleven Art class are in trouble after producing drawings which were very rude indeed without being technically brilliant. They have all been given detention for a week and threatened with suspension if any further obscene drawings are found on the school premises. (Was Rodin given detention?) A number of parents have also complained (including Dad).

Miss Ziggle summons us to the Art room and gives us a lecture about approaching the subject matter in a mature manner, and the necessity of producing good drawings without lending unnecessary emphasis to certain parts of the human anatomy. But it would seem that even Dad's letter of complaint has done nothing to put her off, because our next assignment is to interpret Rodin's *The Kiss* in different media, producing a three-dimensional result (the mind boggles). We are to work on this project in pairs.

Miss Ziggle takes Mark to one side and tells him that his work is going to have to improve dramatically if he is to stand a chance of getting through the exam. I feel sorry for him, but my heart is beating fast because Rob is looking at my drawing, which is pinned up on the wall beside his. (Because he is so talented he has got away with producing work which would have got the rest of us thrown out of St Rhubarb's!)

Rob turns to me and smiles. 'I really like your drawing!' (Oh, WOW. He is so natural – and sincere. My kneecaps wobble like jellyfish.) 'But I don't know why Mark's doing Art, do you? He's rubbish!' (I am taken aback by this unnecessary comment, especially since it is possible that Mark may have overheard. Is it possible – I hardly dare to even think it – that Rob fancies me and is jealous of whatever is left of my relationship with Mark??!)

'Alex – shall we work on this next thing together?' Rob asks. 'I think you and I could make a really great *The Kiss*.'

(Yes. I think so too. Given half the chance.)

'Meet you after school tomorrow?' he continues. 'You can come round to my place, if you like. I can't manage today, because I've got things to do.'

'Ah.' I have lost the power of coherent speech, but I manage to nod agreement.

Abby gives me a jealous prod in the ribs as we leave the Art room. 'Not fair!' she hisses. 'Not fair!'

'Isn't it time you grew up and learned to control your feelings?' I retort, cruelly.

'Why don't *you* grow up?' says Mark, pushing past

57

and glaring at me. (I give up. How is the creative spirit meant to live and breathe in these conditions? I genuinely believe that when I am with Rob it will be like the meeting of two artistic minds – and, with any luck, the subsequent meeting of two artistic bodies.)

Thursday September 21st

I go round to Rob's house, which is huge, with its own bell-tower. Rob's dad is an actor, and Rob tells me that his parents bought the house when his dad was in a stage adaptation of *The Hunchback of Notre Dame*.

'The bell-tower was really useful when Dad was rehearsing,' Rob explains. 'He was only a gargoyle, but he still likes to get the feel of the whole thing. It's called method acting.'

'Ah.'

'I expect Mum's out, but Dad's probably home. He may be in his caravan. Mum and Dad are sort of separated, so Dad spends a lot of time in the caravan. He's resting at the moment.'

'I won't make a lot of noise.'

'No, I mean he's out of work. He's really depressed. But he's auditioning next week for a part in a new play called *Lady Fandermere's Wind*, which is a spoof on the original play by Oscar Wilde, and it's SERIOUSLY FUNNY. Dad would actually have to fart on stage! We're all hoping he gets the work. It would be his big break.'

FUNNY? NOT IF IT WERE <u>MY</u> DAD...

'Of wind?'

'Ha! Yeah. Funny.'

I try to imagine my own dad farting on stage. I think it is unlikely that the rest of the family, myself included, would be sitting in the front row applauding. It is more likely that we would all have publicly disowned him beforehand. It occurs to me that here is a family even STRANGER than my own, which is saying something.

We are in the kitchen (which is enormous), and Rob's dad suddenly rushes in and flops down on a chair, running his hands through his long black hair in a gesture of utter exasperation and frustration. He appears not to have shaved for several days.

'Hi, Tone,' says Rob. 'My dad's name is Tony, Alex.

So we call him Tone.' He puts an arm round his father's shoulders. 'Shall I get you your pills?'

'Those pills are useless! What I need is beans! How am I meant to rehearse for this play without a single can of beans in the whole house??!'

ROB'S DAD (DEPRESSED)

'I can make you a bowl of chilli with extra beans later,' says a glamorous girl with even longer black hair than Rob's dad. She has just wafted into the kitchen, smelling of expensive perfume, and somehow manages to put her arms round everyone, including me, and kiss them on the cheek in the space of about ten seconds.

'This is Hermione,' says Rob. 'She's my sister. Hermi, this is Alex.'

'It's good to meet you, Alex. I've heard so much about you.' (She has?) 'Must fly – I've got a meeting.'

'Hermi's in PR,' explains Rob. 'We'd better leave Dad alone now. He doesn't like people around when he's depressed. Or rehearsing. Or both.'

'Sorry! I am perfectly useless company at the moment, I'm afraid!' Rob's dad calls out, with a flamboyant gesture of the arm in our direction as we leave the kitchen. I grin, and give him a little wave.

ROB'S BIG SISTER →

MY OWN BIG SISTER

'Come on,' says Rob. 'I want you to meet Isambard.'

Isambard turns out to be Rob's pet iguana. It lives in a large dog-basket in a wired-in area in the laundry room, and it eats a dozen eggs a day, shells and all.

'He likes watercress as well,' says Rob. 'But if he ate too much of it, he'd die.'

'Do you take him for walks?'

'Of course. It's just like having a one-metre-long green dog.'

ISAMBARD

After we have finished taking the one-metre-long green dog for a very long, slow trek round Rob's extensive garden, there is no time left for homework. Rob invites me to come back on Sunday, when we will have a few hours free in the afternoon (he seems to be very busy).

'See you at Tracey's party?' he says.

'Sure.'

Friday September 22nd

I overheard Mum and Dad discussing Rob's family last night. They were talking about his mother.

'Of course,' said Mum, 'she has money.'

(Lucky her! I wonder where she keeps it. I have to keep mine – when I have any – in a number of different hiding-places in my room where my horrible, thieving little brothers can't get their sticky hands on it.) Mum went on to say that Rob's mum's first husband was an elderly millionaire called Horatio Potsworthy, who died several weeks after marrying her, leaving his vast fortune to her.

I am quiet and distracted at school, thinking about yesterday. Rob and his family are so much more interesting and glamorous than my own. Rob himself seems totally laid-back and confident, and he always knows what to say and do (like his sister). I think about Mark, who frequently said and did the wrong thing – and we used to laugh about it together. I wonder what the *real* Rob is like . . . I feel as if I don't really know him yet.

The other girls are fascinated, and some (including Abby) are jealous of what they seem to think is the beginning of a 'relationship' between myself and Rob. I don't know if it is or it isn't. But I'd like it to be. I wish Abby would be pleased for me. I feel irritated that she isn't pleased for me. As for Mark, he is in MEGA-SULK MODE. It is a relief to get to the first lesson, which is English.

Mrs Jolly's face has a distinct greenish hue, so the morning sickness obviously isn't getting any better. (She looks just as bad in the afternoon.)

'Clare has very kindly volunteered to read out a poem she has written,' says Mrs Jolly. 'Clare? If you're ready . . . ?'

'Yes, Mrs Jolly. It's called "The Sea".'

Clare clears her throat and begins:

'The tumultuous rolling sea
Deep as the deepest gloom
Upsurging green!
Swelling, bloating waves,
Throwing up sea spume,
Churning, churning,
Like a vast cavernous washing-machine . . .

'Mrs Jolly? Where are you going?'

Mrs Jolly has made a swift exit from the class. After about a quarter of an hour another teacher comes to inform us that Mrs Jolly has had to go home, as she was not feeling well. But she hopes to be back next week. In the meantime, our homework is to write our own poems, on any subject we like (but *not* the sea).

Saturday September 23rd

Tracey's party! I go round to Abby's house in the afternoon to tell her that her friendship is much more important to me than any boy. But how can I help it if boys keep falling for me? She throws several cushions at me, and after that we have fun getting ready for the party. I have borrowed Big Sissy's Deepest Damson lipstick (she doesn't know – yet – that I have borrowed it, because she has gone out for the day with her boyfriend Diggory).

When we arrive at Tracey's house, the party is already in full swing. Her brother Errol is operating the disco, and the house is in darkness apart from the flashing disco lights. There is also a light in the kitchen, where Tracey's mum and dad are busy preparing food, drinks, etc. (Tracey has them well-trained!)

I scan the darkness for any signs of Rob. Yes! He is there, apparently dancing on his own. Then I observe that four girls are dancing with him – or not with him (it is very hard to tell with Rob). He waves to me across the room. 'Hi, Alex! Come and join us!' (Us? I would prefer it if he said come and join *me*.)

Rowena is alternately dancing in a thoroughly aerobic manner with Edward, and then pedalling hard on her cycling machine, which has been installed in a corner of the room. Mark is reclining on a window seat.

ROWENA IS ...DANCING IN A THOROUGHLY AEROBIC MANNER WITH EDWARD ...

He looks at me with an expression as dark as the rest of the room. I decide to ignore him. An inspirational Gemini butterfly such as myself cannot easily deal with his jealous and possessive Aquarian nature. It was flattering and even exciting to begin with that he felt so strongly about me. Now it is getting annoying. I wonder how I would feel if he found another girl-friend. I think I would feel . . . annoyed.

At eleven o'clock the music is suddenly turned down and Tracey invites us all to join her in the dining-room where there is a fax machine. (Don't ask me why they have a fax machine in the dining-room. Perhaps they like to fax orders for pizza, etc.)

'Dean promised he'd send a special fax just after eleven!' Tracey exclaims excitedly. 'His faxes are so cool. You've just got to come and see!'

We all troop obediently into the dining-room, apart from Rob, who stays behind to check out the disco equipment and chill out. (He is *so* laid-back . . .)

By half past eleven there is still no fax and we are all getting restless.

'Perhaps he's forgotten,' suggests Gary.

'Dean doesn't forget,' replies Tracey, firmly.

Suddenly a fax starts to come through, and we all heave a sigh of relief. But not for long . . .

'What is it?' asks Clare.

Everyone is peering at the sheet of paper which has just come through.

'IT'S A BOTTOM...'

'It looks,' says Gary, 'as though Dean has faxed you a photocopy of his bottom.'

'No,' says Tracey. 'Not my Dean. My Dean wouldn't do something like that.'

'It could just be a smudge,' says Freddy.

'It could be anything,' says Louise.

'No,' says Gary, speaking with the voice of experience. 'It's a bottom.' (This is not the exact word he uses, but you should be aware that your younger brother or sister may get hold of this diary and read it. If they are anything like MY younger siblings, they WILL.)

'Wait a minute! There's another page coming through. It's got Dean's writing on it. He's got beautiful writing! He . . . oh.'

We are all looking at the fax. It says: *Hi, Tracey! I've had three pineapple cocktails and I don't know what I'm doing. But I do know I've met someone else and her name is Julianne. Sorry. I'll never forget you. Cheers. Dean.*

Tracey makes a sort of choking noise and rushes upstairs. We hear her bedroom door slam. There is an awkward and embarrassed silence. Several people clear their throats, and we hear a clock strike twelve. It is time for the boys to turn into pumpkins and disappear.

Sunday September 24th

A.M.

I am very tired after a subdued sleep-over at Tracey's house. After the boys had left, her dad went around locking all the doors and windows (he was obviously afraid that the boys might try to get back in).

We went upstairs to talk to Tracey and offer our shoulders to be cried on but she told us all (her mum included) to go away, informing us that she hated her life.

So we all slept downstairs in the living-room, where there was a very limited amount of the usual gossip and giggling. We all expressed our opinions of Dean, which were not complimentary. Soon silence fell, broken only by the sound of distant sobbing from Tracey's room and the steady, rhythmical whirring of the cycling machine (Rowena couldn't sleep, so she

68

decided to give her leg muscles a work-out).

In the morning Tracey felt sufficiently better to allow us into her room to comfort her. We all sat on the bed and took turns putting our arms round her. Unfortunately this made her cry again. Then the emotion of it got too much for the rest of us and we all started crying. Tracey's mum said she thought maybe we were tired and we should go home to rest.

Now I am home, but not for long. I will soon be setting off for Rob's house.

There is time to have a bath, wash my hair, reapply make-up and try to lose that 'slept-over' look. Big Sissy hammers on the bathroom door, demanding the safe return of her lipstick. I splurge some more on to my lips in a hurry before handing it back to her on my way out.

'Going out again? We hardly ever see you, dear!' exclaims Mum. (This is a slight exaggeration. I think I am at home far too much. Perhaps it is wishful thinking on Mum's part.)

'Don't forget your homework!' Dad (The Voice of Doom) calls out to me. 'You've got exams next year.'

'That's why I'm going out, Dad. I'm going out to do my homework. I'm doing it with Rob. Miss Ziggle said we should.'

There is a look in Dad's eye which suggests that another letter to the school is imminent.

P.M.

Rob's family is in the kitchen, and Isambard the iguana is on the table with his nose in a large salad bowl, finishing off a few shreds of lettuce and watercress. Rob's dad is eating baked beans out of a saucepan. He still hasn't shaved.

'For god's sake, Antony!' booms a large lady in a colourful gown, wearing what appears to be a turban on her head. (She bears an uncanny resemblance to Mystic Marge.) 'If you're intending to rehearse for this damn play, at least have the decency to go to your caravan.'

'Your wish is my command, my little sprig of cherry blossom!' replies Rob's dad, and he exits from the

ROB'S MUM (AN UNCANNY RESEMBLANCE TO MYSTIC MARGE ...)

kitchen with a flamboyant wave to the rest of us.

'Alex – meet my mama!' says Rob, in a mock serious tone.

'Charmed! Charmed!' booms Rob's mum. 'Call me Anouska Marie. My father was French and my mother was a Russian princess.' She extends a heavily be-ringed and bejewelled hand to me and I wonder if I ought to kneel down and kiss it.

'Just call her Annie,' says Rob. 'Like the rest of us.'

'Can't stand the name!' booms his mother. 'Names should *never* be shortened! For instance, you are Roberto, after your Italian great-uncle . . .'

'Come on, Annie,' says Rob (Roberto?). 'Chill out. You've got a big day tomorrow. Mum's in charge of a major art collection, and tomorrow it's being moved to new premises in London, as part of a development which cost over forty billion pounds.'

'Wow!' (No wonder Rob's mum has loads of money. I imagine her with forty billion pounds stuffed under her bed – or under her turban, which would have to be enormous . . .)

'You must have heard of the Potsworthy Collection?' continues Rob.

'Er . . .'

'It's the largest collection of multi-dimensional, post-modern destructuralist art in the world. One exhibit alone takes up more than six thousand square metres of floor space. A purpose-built glass warehouse had to be constructed, with special anti-radiation blinds in case of nuclear attack.'

'I . . . I like art, too.' (This is all I can think of to say, although I am raging inwardly at the ludicrous waste of money, when there are so many people starving in the world. But I do not feel inclined to argue with Rob's mother . . .)

'For god's sake!' exclaims Annie suddenly. (Is it something I said? Can she read my mind?) 'Take that damn iguana out of here! Its incessant munching is getting on my nerves. And it has a wind problem. I've got enough of that sort of thing coming from your father at the moment.'

← MILLENNIUM DOME-STYLE

HER TURBAN WOULD HAVE TO BE ENORMOUS...

'Don't be too hard on Tone, Annie. He's pretty depressed.'

'He'd be even more depressed if he wasn't married to me. I support him. He hasn't got a bean.'

'He's got quite a few, actually. Baked beans. Chilli beans . . .'

72

Rob and Annie laugh uproariously. I manage a weak grin (I am beginning to feel sorry for Tone . . .).

Rob and I spend the rest of the afternoon taking Isambard for another leisurely stroll around the garden. We pass Tone's gypsy caravan, from which are erupting various noises (PHARPP! PHARRRP!!!) interspersed with a few swear words. We still haven't done our Art homework. I express a small amount of concern about this.

'Hey, chill out!' says Rob. 'You're not the sort who gets in a stress about homework, are you?'

'Er, oh no! NO.'

'We'll do it tomorrow. I'm busy this evening. But I've got time tomorrow afternoon after school. We'll do it then.'

'Sure. OK. Fine.'

Monday September 25th

Rob looks a little pale today, and I ask him if everything is all right.

'Tone's in hospital.'

'Oh my god. What happened?'

'He was rehearsing for *Lady Fandermere's Wind* in his caravan until late last evening, and then he decided to light a cigarette, and there was this massive explosion, and the caravan was just blown apart . . .'

'Smoking isn't good for you.'

'So he's in hospital, wrapped in bandages. It must've

been bad. He looks like an Egyptian mummy, but he's still hoping to get to the audition on Wednesday . . .'

I feel sorry for Tone, although I am concerned that he is responsible for blowing a massive hole in the ozone layer. I am also worried that the play *Lady Fandermere's Wind* is going to contribute indirectly to global warming, especially if it has a long run in the West End.

Abby keeps asking what is going on between me and Rob. I tell her quite honestly that I don't know.

'Then you must ask him!' she says.

'I must?'

'Of course you must! You have a right to know whether he really likes you, or if he's just stringing you along.'

Abby is right. She has a way of putting things which have been bothering me into words. I decide to talk to Rob this evening.

Rob and I are sitting at the kitchen table. His mum is in London moving the Potsworthy Collection (I hope she doesn't drop anything – WHOOPS! There goes another seven billion pounds . . .) and Hermi is visiting Tone in hospital. (Rob tells me that she has taken in a dozen family-size cans of beans for him, so I hope the hospital has had the good sense to put him in a room on his own.)

Rob informs me that we are going to construct our

three-dimensional *The Kiss* out of nails held together with string and strong glue. I just nod and try to look cool. (**Note:** too much nodding of the head is uncool. But I can't seem to help it. Rob makes me nervous.)

I decide to come straight out with it.

'Rob . . . ?'

'Yes?'

'I . . .'

'Hold on to those nails. No, not THOSE nails! That's better. I'm going to tie them together with string.'

'Rob . . . ?'

'Yes? Where's the glue? You're not concentrating, Alex. The big nail is meant to stick out at right-angles. That's the whole point. And those two rusty nails are meant to cross over, like two lives crossing each other at a certain point. And I want that big screw sticking out at the top . . .'

'Rob . . . ?'

THE MEETING OF TWO ARTISTIC MINDS...

'WHAT DO YOU WANT??! Now you've dropped the whole thing! It's a disaster. We'll never get it done. So what do you want?'

'Nothing.'

Tuesday September 26th

Rob and I managed to get our nail construction finished last night, but it was a lot more difficult than applying false nails (which is saying something!). Rob was in a foul mood by the time we finished (so much for not getting stressed by homework!). I did not feel that it was the right time to ask him how he felt about me.

Miss Ziggle likes our construction very much, and invites the rest of the class to gaze upon it. It is clear that Rob is her favourite, and can therefore do no wrong. (There can be no other reason why a fully-grown woman would get ecstatic about a pile of nails, string and glue.)

Mark has brought in a lump of clay which bears a passing resemblance to a hippopotamus's backside. Miss Ziggle looks at it. Then she looks at Mark, and says: 'Oh dear.' That is all she says. (Why doesn't she help him? I am not sure if I like Miss Ziggle. I don't believe it – I'm feeling protective towards Mark! He doesn't deserve it.)

OH DEAR...

IT BEARS A PASSING RESEMBLANCE TO A HIPPOPOTAMUS'S BOTTOM...

Wednesday September 27th

Abby is cross with me for not confronting Rob. I promise her that I will have another go during the lunch break, so I go to sit at the same table beside him.

'Rob . . . ?'

'Alex.'

'What's your star sign?' (My best chat-up line!!! I know. I know. I'm sad.)

'Oh god, you don't believe in all that stuff, do you?' (Now I feel REALLY STUPID.) Rob continues, 'If you must know, it's Pisces.'

'Oh.' (I once knew a Piscean called Kevin. And he wasn't very nice. But I make a quick recovery . . .)

'Wow, that's amazing! I'm a Gemini, and Pisces and Gemini are a REALLY good combination!' (This may not be true, but it serves my purpose to pretend it is.)

'You don't say.'

'Rob . . . ?'

I ONCE KNEW A PISCEAN CALLED KEVIN

'Yes, Alex . . .'

'Doyoulikeme?' (It all comes out in a rush.)

Rob opens up the egg and cress sandwich on his plate, removes the cress, wraps it in a napkin and stuffs it in his pocket. 'I'm having a party next month. Do you want to come?' (This isn't the answer I was hoping for, but perhaps it is his way of telling me he likes me.) Rob continues: 'It's a sort of Hallowe'en party. But everyone celebrates Hallowe'en on October the thirty-first, which is really boring. So I'm going to celebrate it on Friday October the thirteenth. That's thirty-one backwards, you see. And it's a dead unlucky day, if you happen to be superstitious. But I'm not.'

'Right. OK. Yes. That'd be great! I'd love to come.'

Thursday September 28th

Rob comes dancing towards me across the canteen, waving a sandwich in the air. He is wildly excited about something. 'He's got it! He's got the part! My dad's going to be in *Lady Fandermere's Wind*! I can't believe it!' (Rob is so excited that he even forgets to call his father by his first name.) 'We all went out last night for a curry. Dad had a vindaloo. And LOADS of poppadums! It was really nice to see Tone and Annie together, having a good time. Don't suppose it'll last, though.' Rob suddenly looks sad.

(NOW is the moment when I should reach out and touch Rob's hand, our eyes will meet, a mighty orchestra will begin to play . . .)

'This sandwich tastes like mouldy cotton wool! I'm off to get some chips.' (Too late. The moment has passed . . .)

Mrs Jolly is about the same colour as Isambard the iguana (green). Wearily she slumps in a chair at the front of the class and gazes out across the sea of faces (unfortunate turn of phrase) with eyes which dimly recognise them as belonging to the Year Eleven English class. One of the boys thoughtfully places a bucket (left behind by one of the cleaners) beside her chair.

'Thank you, Freddy. That's very kind of you,' she whispers. With a tremendous effort of will she forces a truly ghastly grin. 'Today I would like you to read out the poems you have written. Rob – would you begin, please?' She stares at him, and then looks away in a manner which suggests that the colour of his hair (green) is making her feel worse.

THANKYOU, FREDDY— THAT'S VERY KIND...

Rob clears his throat. 'I've written a poem to celebrate my dad getting a part in a major new play.'

'Very good. Carry on.'

'Right. It's called "The Actor":

'The great actor stands centre stage
He doesn't look bad, considering his age.
Like a colossus, with feet wide apart
And then he lets rip with a colossal . . .'

'Rob! That's enough! I would like to remind the rest of the class that poetry is a serious subject, and that you should use it as a vehicle for expressing feelings and thoughts which are difficult to convey in other ways.'

Exhausted after this long speech, Mrs Jolly leans back in her chair, gasping slightly like a stranded fish.

She points to Gary, indicating that he should be the next to read out his poem. Gary leaps to his feet, extracting a crumpled sheet of paper from his pocket.

'Poor presentation,' murmurs Mrs Jolly, in a sad, defeated little voice.

'I've called it "Fear".'

'Good.'

' "Fear".

'Fear is a black thing
Which falls on you.
Fear makes your stomach churn
And then you have to rush to the bathroom.
But you can't find the bathroom!
Which is pretty frightening
When you're desperate.
Then you think you're going to throw up
A great whoosh of semi-digested . . .'

Mrs Jolly has left the room. Another teacher comes to take over the class and informs us that Mrs Jolly has had to go home again. Rob and Gary are given detention and the rest of us are issued with a stern warning to behave in a more sensitive and considerate manner in future. (This is unfair. None of the girls, and only a few of the boys, found Gary's poem at all funny. It didn't even scan. But I feel sorry for Rob. He was only writing the truth!)

Saturday September 30th

Rosie's fourth birthday party! There are about ten little guests (it seems as though there are about four times that number). The girls are wearing party dresses and the boys are looking smart and sweet in little shirts and ties (BLESS!). After about five minutes of being barged and jostled and pulled at from every direction, I have had ENOUGH. (Mum said she wanted to keep the party short, and I *did* tell her that in my opinion ten minutes would be long enough . . .) I remember that I have a lot of homework, and am about to retire to my room when Mum hauls me back and insists that I HELP. (Whatever happened to the parental preoccupation with homework and exams? It seems to have been put to one side . . .)

My last, despairing request is to be allowed to make one phonecall. I can hardly make myself heard above the happy noises, bangs, crashes and the screams and cries of one or two of the guests trying to kill each other. But I manage to get through to Abby and appeal to her to answer my SOS. She agrees to come round, and it is a great relief to see her.

'A kiddies' birthday party! What fun!' she exclaims, as she comes through the door. Then a low-flying bowl of red jelly hits her at waist level and she becomes more aware of the direness of the situation.

Abby and I each find a shy, quiet little girl and sit

down with them on our laps. But this is not good enough for Mum, who looks flustered.

'Alex – will you start Pass the Parcel? And please stop Duncan and Peter from fighting! Abby – be a dear and help me in the kitchen – they all want more drinks!'

The party is soon in full swing. Most of the guests are dancing to Rosie's favourite tape, a rap version of 'Baa Baa Black Sheep' and other nursery rhymes. One of the shy, quiet little girls is howling because Duncan knocked her down (and she never wanted to come in the first place because she hates it here, as she confides in me while I am giving her a cuddle). I am now covered in smears of chocolate cake and red jelly, and Rosie has stuck a party hat on my head (I think she has stuck it to my head with jam, but I am not sure). There is a loud knock at the door . . .

I open the door, and there is Rob . . . (OH NO. THIS IS NOT HAPPENING. I AM STILL WEARING MY PARTY HAT.)

THIS IS NOT HAPPENING...

'Nice hat!' says Rob with a grin. 'I love kids' parties. Can I come in? I saw the balloons outside your door and thought PARTY TIME!'

'How did you know I live here?'

'Ah! I know everything. I've got Isambard with me. Is that OK?' Before I can say anything, Rob and Isambard (who is on a lead) have entered the room where the party is taking place. All the children freeze in a way which would have won them a prize in Musical Statues.

'It's a dragon,' says Duncan, quietly.

The two shy, quiet little girls burst into tears and Abby and I scoop them up and do our best to reassure them.

'Is it a dragon?' asks Peter.

'No, it's an iguana. You can stroke him, if you like. Very gently.'

Isambard is a Big Hit. Rosie feeds him two egg and cress sandwiches, and Duncan shoves a slice of chocolate cake into Isambard's mouth before anyone can stop him. The children take turns at walking Isambard round the room on the lead. Mum wants to know if he is house-trained. We all ignore her.

Rob leaves at the same time as the other guests, taking a balloon and a slice of cake with him. I am left wondering why he came round. It is as though he really *did* just want to come to a children's party . . . what a sweet guy!

Sunday October 1st

Abby is in NO doubt about Rob's reasons for coming round. 'He FANCIES you, Alex! Coming to Rosie's party was just an excuse to see you.'

'Yes, but . . .'

'No! Don't say anything! I'm jealous.'

We are upstairs in my bedroom, chatting and reading *YEZZ!* magazine.

'But you're going out with James,' I point out.

'I know that. But I wouldn't mind if Rob fancied me!'

'Boys are always fancying you! Now it's my turn.'

Further debate is prevented by a loud knock at the door.

'Alex!' Mum calls in her silly, trilly voice. 'It's your friend Rob and his . . . lizard thing.'

Rob has come to ask if we would like to go with him to take the Lizard Thing for a walk. Abby gives me a knowing look and I poke her in the ribs with my elbow.

'It's the igubanana!' exclaims Rosie, rushing up to pat Isambard and offer him a pretend cup of tea from her tea set.

My brothers are also fascinated by the creature, and Daniel tries to show off by saying that he knows someone who has six iguanas AND a python, and his friend's iguanas are much bigger than this one. (I HATE it when my brothers show off.)

'I like your family,' says Rob, generously, as we walk the igubanana along the pavement.

'They're OK.'

'What do you call your ma and pa?'

'Ah.' (Their names are Hank and Petunia, but this is far too embarrassing to admit to anyone. But Rob will think I'm boring if I tell him that I call them Mum and Dad.)

'Er, I call them . . . Tilly and Lawrence!' (A lorry has just gone past with these names emblazoned on its side. Abby gives me a look and I grin nervously.)

'Lovely names.'

We turn a corner and, once again, nearly collide with Mark coming the other way. This time Mark is walking Dogbert. We try to pass each other without acknowledging each other's existence, but Dogbert has other ideas. He decides to check out Isambard's bottom with his nose (he obviously wants to find out if the one-metre-long green dog really is a dog and, secondly, if it should happen to be a FEMALE one-metre-long green dog . . .). Isambard is outraged. He spins around with

DOGBERT MEETS ISAMBARD

amazing speed, opens his mouth wide and hisses fiercely at Dogbert. Dogbert rushes off at high speed, yelping and dragging Mark along behind him. Both Mark and Dogbert disappear round the corner.

'Sound chap, Mark,' says Rob. (I think Rob has a kind heart. I'm sure he didn't mean what he said about Mark when we were in the Art room.)

The rest of the walk is uneventful. Rob says goodbye to us outside my house because he has to get home and do some things (he doesn't volunteer a lot of information). Dad is in the front garden worrying a small bush with a pair of shears. 'Nice work, Lawrence!' Rob calls out to him over the hedge. Then he wanders away, leaving Dad gazing after him with a puzzled expression on his face.

Monday October 2nd

Rob has had his left eyebrow pierced!

'Hermi did it for me. She'll pierce any part of your body, if you ask her.' (I don't think I shall be asking her. But I am becoming increasingly worried that my appearance is far too boring to interest someone like Rob . . . What can I do? What would it be

ROB WITH EYEBROW PIERCED BY COOL BIG SISTER (JUST DON'T LET HER NEAR ME . . .)

like to have a big sister like Hermi? I imagine Big Sissy bearing down on me with a needle/staple gun or hole punch – NIGHTMARE! She would get the hole in the wrong place . . . I am glad, on the whole – ha ha – that she isn't like Hermi. I like her just as she is – most of the time . . .)

Mark is sitting next to me during Geography (Rob does not do Geography. It is BORING, in his opinion). At first Mark makes a point of not speaking to me. Then he can't restrain himself any longer . . .

'It was completely irresponsible and stupid for you and your green-haired FRIEND' (he says it with such contempt!) 'to take that dangerous creature out for a walk! Dogbert was terrified!'

'Isambard isn't dangerous!'

'Isambard??! What kind of name is that??!'

'It's a lovely name.'

'No it's not. It's stupid. Like your FRIEND. And his eyebrow looks stupid. And his hair looks like a giant just sneezed on his head.'

I am trembling all over, and on the point of pushing Mark off his chair. (I shall set Rowena on him, if he goes on like this. She has reached the advanced level in several martial arts, including kick-boxing.)

'Well, he likes YOU!' I retort, hoping to shame him.

'He's a poser. I wouldn't trust his friendship.'

(I am now too angry to speak. This is just as well,

because Mr Fisher the Geography teacher is staring hard in our direction . . .)

When the lesson is over, Mark says to me: 'You don't even care about Dogbert!' (I don't believe it! First he is jealous of Dogbert, and now he is using him as an emotional weapon. Although the thought of using Dogbert as any kind of weapon is bizarre . . .)

Tuesday October 3rd

Tracey is back with Zak. It seems that he has a heart of gold, even if he has feet of cheese (she jilted him because his feet smelled too bad), and he is there to comfort her in her hour of need.

She is lucky. I fear that Mark is losing it completely (due to his inability to harness strong emotions and channel them in a more positive direction, as Mystic Marge has frequently advised lovelorn Geminis, Pisceans, Aquarians, etc. to do). He is certainly in danger of losing me. Or has he already lost me? All these questions are too difficult to answer, and I decide to forget boys and concentrate on my Art instead (and I must not forget that I have exams next year, etc. etc. yawn yawn zzzzzzzzz . . .).

Miss Ziggle wants us to go away and do a painting on the theme of 'Rejection'. I decide that I will paint myself turning my back on ALL BOYS (or as many as I can fit on the sheet of paper). They will all look suitably rejected.

MY PAINTING OF REJECTION (OF ALL BOYS)

I go round to Abby's house after school for top-level discussions about how to make my appearance more interesting and attractive. (**Note:** I am doing this for MYSELF, not to attract ANY BOY . . .) We decide that we will meet up and maybe go into town on Saturday to see what we can sort out.

'I'm thinking of having another hole in each ear,' I tell Abby. 'Do you think your mum would do them for me?' (Abby's mum is a beautician.)

'No, she won't. She's in a mood at the moment and she just says "no" to everything.'

It is just as well that Abby and I are two such sensible (sometimes) and well-adjusted individuals, since we are always having to deal with moody mothers . . . Thankfully, I am no longer distracted by the subject of boys . . .

Wednesday October 4th
Only nine days to go till Rob's party!

Thursday October 5th
Only eight days to go till Rob's party!

Friday October 6th
Only a week to go till Rob's party!

Saturday October 7th
I go round to Abby's house to draw up a plan to make us both look more interesting (Abby doesn't see why she should help me if I don't help her, which is fair enough). Half an hour later we are ready to put our plan into practice. Here it is:

Plan
1) Dye hair. Suggested colours: dark green, light green, grass-green. Or blue. Possibly just streaks rather than whole head.
2) Get fashionable mini hair decorations to add interest to hair. Hair does not get more interesting than this.
3) Try out different make-up. Save money by borrowing Alex's sister's make-up. Save more money by getting Abby's mum to cut and style Alex's interesting hair (if she is not in a mood). Abby already has a fabby new hairstyle, courtesy

of her mum (the advantages of having a beautician as a mother!).

4) Have second hole put in all four ears (that's Abby and me). Save even MORE money by appealing to Abby's mum to do this for us (make nice cup of tea with biscuits before asking her).

5) Have nose pierced, also both eyebrows AND navel.

6) Delete the above.

'What's wrong with having our noses, eyebrows and navels pierced, Abby?'

'I don't know. Mum says it's dangerous. The risk of infection. Not that you have to do what she says, of course. But she might get in an even worse mood if we did.'

'OK, we'll stick to ears.'

We prepare a tray with a mug of tea (milk, no sugar), a little plate of biscuits (tastefully arranged) and even a small vase with a late rose from the garden in it, and take it to Abby's mum.

'OK. So what do you two want?' (Parents can be so cynical!)

We tell her.

Of course, Abby's mum has to phone MY mum, to ask if it is all right. I hear Mum's voice on the phone saying: 'I suppose I'd better say yes. Alex will only get in a mood if I say no . . .'

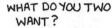

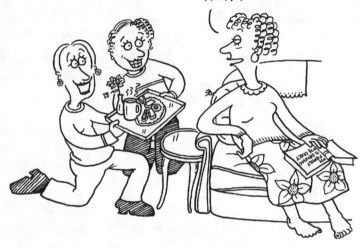

PARENTS CAN BE SO CYNICAL!

We are pleased with our newly pierced ears. Abby's mum (who seems to be in a GOOD mood!) takes us into town, where we find some green hair dye (explaining to Abby's mum that it is for a party), some very pale, almost white make-up (good for UnHallowe'en parties!), a couple of toe-rings and a nail-piercing kit (I hope my nails grow long enough before next Saturday! I think I have some false nails left . . .).

Sunday October 8th

With trembling hands I open the pack containing the green hair dye. Abby and I have locked ourselves in the bathroom at my house. We were not meant to use the dye until next Saturday (for Rob's party – the green party, ha ha) but I cannot wait. (I have always been in favour of 'going green' – ha ha again. I may as well show my solidarity with green issues by turning the same colour – just my hair, I mean. I'll leave Mrs Jolly to go for the whole-body green look . . .) Abby has decided that she doesn't want green hair, but she has offered to help me.

An hour or so later I am startled by the effect. I have bright green streaks in my hair! It is certainly interesting. Abby and I both have green fingers, despite the gloves which were thoughtfully provided with the dye. I also have one ear which is tinged green.

Now it is necessary to come out of the bathroom.

'Alex's hair has gone mouldy!' shrieks Brother Number Two (I wish I had stayed in the bathroom).

'I preferred your natural colour, dear,' says Mum. 'Such pretty hair.'

'You'll be in trouble at school,' says Dad. 'You can't take exams with hair like that.'

I point out to them patiently that Rob has green hair, and no one seems too worried about it. Dad goes off, muttering, to write another letter to the school . . .

Monday October 9th

My hair is much admired at school, although Mrs Jolly looks distinctly queasy. Gary is fascinated by my green ear. Rob, on the other hand, makes no comment at all.

Later on I find him in the Art room, working on his painting of 'Rejection'. He has drawn a sad-looking figure all hunched up and huddled into a doorway. He asks me what colour I think he should use for the door in the background.

'Green,' I reply. 'DEFINITELY GREEN. GREEN is a good colour. You can't go wrong with GREEN.'

'I don't agree,' he says, without looking up. 'No, I think it's got to be a dark bluish-grey.'

I heave a sigh and turn my attention to some drawings I am working on. I have been asked by the school to draw some figures to be used in the school prospectus. I have to draw a typical Rhubarbian (female) and another typical Rhubarbian (male), and a typical teacher. It is flattering that my drawing skills have been recognised, but I am not sure what to do. I have a go at drawing the typical Rhubarbian (male). I have been told

MY DRAWINGS OF TYPICAL RHUBARBIAN (MALE) FOR ST RHUBARB'S SCHOOL PROSPECTUS

MUCH BETTER (BUT REJECTED BY HEAD TEACHER)

to make the figures look smart, so I give my Rhubarbian a neat side-parting. This looks completely mad, so I rub it out and give him normal hair instead. I would like to give him green hair, but the drawings have to be in black and white. I draw a female teacher, but she has a strange expression on her face, as if she is about to throw up (so it might be Mrs Jolly!). Back to the drawing board . . .

Tuesday October 10th

Only three days to go till Rob's party! EEEEEEEEEK!!! (I make this noise when I'm excited.)

I ask Mum to take up my school skirt because it is far too long (halfway down my thigh!). She refuses, and says that as I grow, the skirt will get shorter. (**Note:** This is an example of maternal logic, which only makes sense to mothers.) I argue that I can't wait that long. I want a shorter skirt NOW. (If I wait to grow as tall as I need to be for the skirt to be as short as I want it to be, it is likely that I will have left school by then, in which case I am *most* unlikely to want to wear my school skirt! Unless I have turned into a seriously weird person. And if I have, it will be all my family's fault!) (**Note:** How much more does Mum expect me to grow, anyway? I don't want to tower over Rob! Or Mark.)

Wednesday October 11th

Only two days to go till Rob's party! EEEEEEEEEEEEEEEK!!!

AS YOU GROW, DEAR, THE SKIRT WILL GET SHORTER...

MATERNAL LOGIC

Thursday October 12th

Only one day to go ... EEEEEEEEEEEEEEEEE-EEEEEEK!!!

Friday October 13th

EEEEEEEEEEEEEEEEEEEEEEEEEEEEEEEEEEEEEEE-EEEK!!!!!

Sorry. I go round to Abby's house straight after school so that we can get ready. I have brought the white make-up and the Deepest Damson lipstick (Big Sissy has decided that it doesn't suit her and has *given* it to me! She is WONDERFUL ...).

We achieve a dramatic (and SCARY!) look, suitable for an UnHallowe'en party. Then we apply false nails, green and black nail varnish, and have fun with the nail-piercing kit. We are wearing mainly black, with silver glitter on our shoulders. We pretend to be witches' cats, hissing and snarling and taking little swipes at each other with our claws. Then we sit quietly on Abby's bed, realising that we are ready several hours too early.

Several hours later . . .

We arrive at Rob's party. The front of the house and several trees in the garden are festooned with green lights (green for GO! GO! GO!) which gives the whole place an eerie feel. Someone is tolling on the bell in the bell-tower. The eeriness is increased when we are met at the front door by Rob's sister Hermi wearing stark white make-up, deep purple eye make-up and black lipstick. (Our own attempts at looking scary pale into insignificance.) Her long black hair adds to the effect – she looks like a witch!

CALL ME MORTICIA!

←THE SIGHT OF ROB'S SISTER CAUSES GREEN HAIR TO STAND ON END, ADDING GREATLY TO OVERALL EFFECT...

'Call me Morticia!' she says.

'A lovely name!' booms Rob's mum, sweeping past in a gown with a black feather boa wound

← DEAD CROW EFFECT

← HOW MANY BLACK OSTRICHES, CHICKENS, DUCKS, GEESE ETC GAVE UP THEIR LIVES TO MAKE THIS? (I HOPE IT'S FAKE ...)

BLACK FISH NET GOWN

round her shoulders (I wonder how many black ostriches/chickens/ducks/geese, etc. gave up their lives to make this? I hope it's fake!). She is wearing an extraordinary black and red hat, decorated with black feathers (it looks like a crow has had a nasty accident).

'My love! You look radiant! Like the first night I met you!' Rob's dad is wearing a pair of fluorescent pink bathing shorts and nothing else. (Did I mention that this was a STRANGE family ... ?)

The house is full of people of all ages, most of whom I don't know (and neither does Abby). We wander into the kitchen and find Isambard walking slowly round the table. Someone has attached a fluffy green wig to his head (now he looks like a one-metre-long green poodle – possibly the scary Poodle of the Baskervilles!). Rob's mum invites us to help ourselves to food.

ONE-METRE-LONG GREEN POODLE
(DRESSED UP AS SCARY POODLE OF THE BASKERVILLES!)

'There are slices of black pudding, black bean salad, garlic bread to ward off the vampires, baked beans to ward off everyone (just ask Tone!), black Melba toast – Tone burned it, I'm afraid – and heaps of black grapes and green jelly! Just help yourselves! And please don't feed the iguana.' (I decide that I am not THAT hungry.)

There is a live band playing in the garden. They are called The Undead (but they are a *live* band, if you see what I mean . . .). A few people have kicked off their shoes and are dancing on the lawn. One of them is Rob.

'Who's the girl? He's dancing with a girl. I've never seen him dance with anyone before. He's put his arm round her! Oh no, they're coming in this direction . . .'

'Hi, Alex! Hello, Abby! Glad you could make it. Help yourselves to drinks, won't you?'

'I'm soooooo thirsty!' exclaims the Unknown Girl. 'I'm off to get a drink, Robbo . . .' (Robbo?)

'Who was that?' I can't help asking when she has gone.

'Oh, just some girl.' (Great.)

Suddenly a dazzlingly beautiful girl with long blonde hair glides (yes – she glides) up to us and puts her arm round Rob. 'Hi, Robbie!' (Robbie?) 'Come and dance with me!'

'Sure, babe.'

'Who was that?' Abby asks, when Rob and the Second Unknown One have gone to dance.

'Oh, just some girl,' I reply, drily. (The rest of me is turning green with envy to match my hair, nails, etc.)

Abby and I end up dancing together. (No one has asked us to dance. We don't have any friends. We're sad . . .)

'Why don't we ask Rob to dance?' Abby suggests. 'Although I think it's a bit much that he didn't invite James.'

'Or Mark.'

'Shall we ask him anyway?'

Just as we are about to do this, another girl comes up to Rob and gives him an enormous hug. 'Come and dance with me, Robs!' (Robs?)

Abby and I dance the rest of the night away . . . together. The evening ends with an impressive display of green fireworks and we all have a green sparkler (I suppose it wouldn't be cool to have fireworks on November the fifth, like everyone else . . .). Finally we toast green and black marshmallows.

When Abby's mum comes to collect us (this is

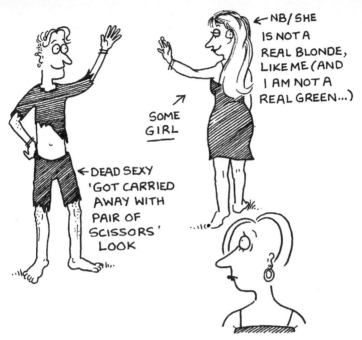

MEGA UNCOOL, but there was nothing we could do to stop her – Abby is an only child and her parents are protective – unlike mine, who would probably send Big Sissy or Diggory to fetch me, if they bothered at all) we are given a party bag and a black or green balloon and a slice of vampire cake with black icing and green filling to take home. Morticia – I mean Hermi – is in charge of party bags. Rob is nowhere to be seen. I ask Hermi where he is.

'Oh, I expect he's somewhere upstairs with Alison.'

'Who . . . ?'

'Come on, Alex,' says Abby, taking me firmly by the arm. 'It's time to go home.'

Before we can get into her mum's car, James appears out of nowhere. 'So. You went to Rob's party. You didn't even tell me you were going. But I thought I might find you here. I wasn't invited.'

'We'll talk about it another time,' says Abby. 'It's too late now.'

Abby and I exchange glances. We are *both* dealing with jealous boyfriends!

Abby's mum says in an annoyingly bright and cheerful voice: 'Good party, girls?' (This is almost as bad as the silly, trilly 'There's-SOMEONE-at-the-door' voice.)

'Great!' I reply. (I am always bright and polite to other people's parents!)

Abby just grunts (which is a more accurate reflection of the way I am really feeling . . .).

Saturday October 14th

I am depressed. As far as I am concerned, Friday the thirteenth lived up to its reputation. I now realise that I mean nothing to Rob. I am just 'some girl'. Mark never made me feel as though I was just some girl. He made me feel special. My eyes fill with tears. AAAAAARGH!!! (And who is Alison?)

I phone Abby, and ask if I can come round. She says yes, and tells me that Tracey, Rowena and Clare are coming round, too, for a Boyfriend Crisis Conference. This gives me a chance to ask them all what they think

I should do, and Abby has a chance to ask us what she should do about James.

Note: Shouldn't we be deciding for ourselves? It occurs to me that too much advice from too many people, even if they are good friends, can be confusing. I am the only one who really knows what is going on in my own mind and my own life, even if certain others think they know it all! Abby's attitude to Rob has certainly changed – she now thinks he is unreliable and that Mark is steadier – or does she mean boring? She says that I have been unfair to Mark!!!? And she was the one who encouraged me to put him in his place??! So I am trying to keep a detached attitude to my friends' advice (although it is difficult when they start winding me up!).

When I arrive at Abby's house I am momentarily startled into silence by the sight of Rowena, who has had her long black hair cut off! My friends are full of questions about Rob's party, and they are being rude about him and about his family, probably because they were not invited. I tell them they didn't miss anything. Then I ask them if, in their opinion, I have been a little unkind to Mark. (This is a good way to steer the conversation away from Rob's party, as Abby and I both feel embarrassed about being more or less ignored by Rob all evening. And I don't have to take my friends' advice about Mark. I am just curious to

hear what they have to say, and if they think I have been unfair.)

'Yes! Definitely! Poor Mark! Haven't you even noticed how upset he is? How could you, Alex? He really loves you!' (OK. I wish I hadn't asked. Next question . . .)

'So what do you think I should do?'

'Take up weight-training,' suggests Rowena. 'Or I could probably get you into the rugby team.' (Thanks. No thanks.)

'And what am I going to do about James?' Abby asks. 'He's so jealous of Rob. And it's not as though he needs to be. There's nothing going on.' (True.)

'You've both got to talk to them,' says Tracey. 'If you're good friends, you'll be able to sort things out. Friendship is the most important part of any relationship. Just think about me and Zak. He was there for me when things didn't work out between me and Dean. Dean wasn't my friend. Zak is. And now we couldn't be happier! Especially since I gave him those De-feet Odour-eaters and special deodorising socks.'

'Why don't you write Mark a poem, Alex?' suggests Clare. We all roll around on the floor laughing hysterically at the thought of me writing a poem to Mark.

Sunday October 15th

I spend most of the day writing a poem to Mark. Then I fold it up very small and hide it somewhere at the bottom of my schoolbag in the hope that my brothers will NOT discover it. At least I have a poem to read out in case Mrs Jolly asks me to produce one. I don't think it is too obvious that it is meant for Mark . . .

Monday October 16th

Late afternoon

Did I mention that my beloved big sister Daisy has a mean and sadistic streak? I am mentioning it NOW (in case she is reading this diary). It is bad enough being nagged by Mum or Dad to tidy my room, pick my clothes, books and other stuff up off the floor, get on with my homework, get off the phone, etc. etc. without Big Sissy getting in on the act and nagging me *as well*. She is always throwing her weight around (which is considerable – no apologies this time because she has ANNOYED me). I don't know how Diggory puts up with it. 'Do this, Diggory!' 'Fetch that, Diggory!' 'Aren't you meant to be tidying your room, Alex?' 'Don't you have homework to do, Alex?' 'Alex! Where's my mascara?' (As if I should know!)

So I am forever grateful to Diggory (who has many good points, if you can ignore the wobbling Adam's apple) when he announces his intention of taking Big Sissy to a very exciting (NOT) poetry recital at the library this evening. I heave a deep sigh of relief and contentment at the prospect of a peaceful and undisturbed evening watching TV, relaxing in the bath without Big Sissy hammering on the door, trying out her new Madagascan mud facial mask without interruption, etc.

My happy little mood is shattered when Dad says: 'You could take Alex with you, couldn't you? A poetry recital has got to be good preparation for the English exam next year!'

(THANKS, Dad.)

At this point all my brothers start sniggering, and Daniel says: 'Alex LIKES poetry, don't you, Alex?'

Seb says: 'Who was it FOR, Alex? Was it for Marky-poo?'

Henry adds, unnecessarily: 'We read your poem.' (I DO NOT BELIEVE IT.)

Diggory's normally pale face is unusually flushed with excitement by the time we reach the library. Mine is still bright red with embarrassment and sheer rage at my horrible little brothers – they poke their snotty, spotty noses into EVERYTHING!!!

Diggory tells us that the poet who is going to recite extracts from his latest volume of verse (or worse) is the most exciting poet of our times. His name is Andrew Static.

'And he's totally charismatic!' enthuses Diggory.

'I wanted to stay at home and wash my hair.' (Big Sissy.)

'So did I. It isn't fair!' (Me.)

I notice that Clare is in the audience with her parents.

The most exciting poet of our times turns out to be a

THE MOST EXCITING POET OF OUR TIMES . . .

tall, thin man with unruly long brown hair which stands on end while he is reciting (too much static, I expect). His hair is the most exciting thing about him, and I find it so distracting that it is difficult to concentrate on what he is saying.

'Brilliant! Brilliant!' shouts Diggory, clapping vigorously as Mr Static takes a bow and collapses into a chair, exhausted by the powerful emotions which his hair has been expressing all evening. Clare and her dad, along with several others, ask him to sign copies of his book.

'Can we go home now? I'm feeling tired.' (Big Sissy.)

'Carry me, please. I have expired.' (Me.)

Tuesday October 17th

Will I ever recover from my wild night out with Diggory and Daisy? (Sarcasm.) Tracey and Rowena went to the fair last night with their boyfriends, and keep raving on about the wonderful time they had and how some of the rides were scarEEE and so they had to hug each other tight, etc. etc. yawn, yawn (not really – I am JEALOUS). I decide to keep quiet about my wild night at the library.

'The poetry recital was really good, wasn't it, Alex?' Clare asks, in a voice that I feel is unnecessarily loud for someone who doesn't usually say anything. My friends are all looking at me, as if they don't quite believe what they are hearing.

'Oh, er . . . yes, it was . . . OK.'

'You went to a poetry recital, Alex?'

'I couldn't get out of it. Dad made me go, with Diggory and Daisy.'

'You poor thing.'

'Yes. I hate poetry.'

Wednesday October 18th

'Alex, would you read us your poem?' (We have been studying the balcony scene in Shakespeare's *Romeo and Juliet* for the last half an hour, so it is a hard act to follow.) I clear my throat, and try to read my poem in a voice that suggests that poetry isn't really my thing but there was no way I could get out of it:

'My poem is called "Sorry".

'I'm sorry for the way I behaved
You were drowning and I thought you waved.
I've always cared
I think you know
But I was afraid to let it show.
Friends are important, let's not forget.
Not writing this poem before
Is my one major regret.'

(OK. So the last two lines don't scan. But it comes from the heart.)

'Thank you, Alex!' exclaims Mrs Jolly. 'That's an

amazing poem.' (It must be. It hasn't made her sick.) 'I shall arrange for it to be published in the school magazine as a definite contender for the Jolly Poetry Prize.' (Oh no. Mrs Jolly's pregnancy hormones are affecting her sense of judgement.) 'Would you do one of your drawings to go with it?' (It gets worse.) (And then it gets worse again – Clare is so moved by my poem that she bursts into tears. I can't stand it.)

As we leave the room, Mark says to me grumpily: 'I don't suppose that poem was for me.'

'Actually it was.'

I leave him standing, open-mouthed, in the corridor.

MY POEM HAS A STRANGE
EFFECT ON CLARE

Thursday October 19th

Mark and I are being incredibly polite to each other. But there are some awkward silences when we don't really know what to do or say. (This is almost worse than when we were fighting!)

← ROWENA'S HAIR!
(WHAT HAIR?)

Rowena has had the rest of her hair cut off. But I have decided to keep my hair on (ha ha).

Tuesday October 24th

Mark and I are still being polite. He is soooooooo polite that I want to strangle him (no, sorry, I don't mean that!).

Miss Ziggle likes my painting of 'Rejection'. She agrees that with so many important exams on the horizon, it is a good idea to forget about boys for the time being. (All the boys in the class look disappointed and sadly put away their bottles of Stynx 2000.) She raves about Rob's painting, as usual. (It *is* good.) Then she looks at Mark's work.

'What's going on here, Mark?'

'It's a picture of you rejecting my work because it isn't good enough!'

A few people laugh, and then there is silence.

'I don't think you've got my hair quite right. And the colours are muddy.'

(I HATE it when she puts Mark down like this . . .)

'I think it's brilliant!' I hear myself saying. 'It's clever. And it's funny.'

'OK, Alex. That's enough. Mark needs to work on getting his colours right . . .'

(HAH! I think I have successfully put Miss Ziggle in her place. Bang goes my chance of winning the Art prize – but so what?)

Later on

'Thanks for standing up for me, Alex.'

'That's OK, Mark.'

'No, I mean it. Thank you.'

'I said that's OK.'

'It was good of you. I really wanted to thank you.'

'You have.'

'I mean it.'

'I know.'

'Thanks.'

(AAAAAAAAAAARGH!!!)

I REALLY WANTED TO THANK YOU – I CAN'T THANK YOU ENOUGH..!

HE IS SOOOOOOOO POLITE...

Friday October 27th

Half-term starts HERE! (The moment we get out of school . . .) It is just as well, as Mark and I are STILL being polite, and I don't think I can STAND it much longer . . . I am going to spend half-term in my room, being very rude indeed to my teddy bear (not that he deserves it, but I have to rid of pent-up feelings . . .).

Saturday October 28th

Mark comes round to ask (very politely) if I would like to go for a walk with him and Dogbert. I hear myself say, 'Yes. Thank you. That would be great.' (So much for any alternative plans I may have made . . .)

Friday November 3rd

Half-term is nearly over, and I seem to have spent most of it with Mark, taking Dogbert for long and very polite walks. (Dogbert was rude to an elderly lady's Jack Russell on one occasion, but that doesn't count . . .) I managed to escape to my room one afternoon, and was in the middle of being VERY rude to my teddy bear when Mum walked in, which was EMBARRASSING.

Saturday November 4th

Now that Tone has landed the part (which had become vacant after the previous actor had to retire suffering from exhaustion and deflation), *Lady Fandermere's Wind* looks set to enjoy an even longer run in the West End. It even got a mention in *YEZZ!* magazine, which described it as a 'gas' (does no one care about the ozone layer apart from me?).

I meet Rob out walking Isambard. He can't stop talking about the play and how great his dad was in it.

'We all went to Tone's first night,' he tells me. 'It was mega-exciting when the curtain was raised . . .' (or blown apart?) '. . . and Tone was just, oh wow, so cool, – he really blew me away . . .' (literally?) '. . . and as for the moment when he farted . . .' (I want to say something about 'lowering the Tone' but I decide not to) '. . . you could hear it at the back of the dress circle – it was like a gunshot, and it brought the house down!' (I can imagine – just think what it did to the caravan.) 'We had our own box, of course . . .'

'You had chocolates?'

'No, you idiot. We sat in a box.'

'Weren't there any seats?'

'Alex – you're mad. Anyway, the play is a runaway success. Jill loved it.'

'Who's Jill?'

'Oh, just some girl.' (Of course. Silly of me.)

'Want to help me walk Isambard?'

'OK.'

We turn the corner and – yes, how did you guess? – we meet Mark coming in the other direction with Dogbert. Dogbert freezes, and his hackles rise. He snarls in a very unDogbert-like way. Isambard's mouth opens wide and, if he were a dragon, this is the moment when he would roar and breathe fire all over Dogbert. Fortunately (for Dogbert) he is an iguana, so

all he can manage is a stupid hiss. But this is too much for Dogbert, who is not renowned for his bravery. He turns tail and runs away at high speed, yelping and dragging Mark on the lead after him.

Rob is helpless with laughter. 'Mark is such an idiot!' he exclaims. (He is not as kind as I had thought.) 'Why's he doing Art, Alex? He's hopeless at it! And as for that dog, it's such a boring, ordinary-looking mutt – a bit like Mark, I suppose.'

This is the final straw.

'Mark is NOT boring. He's my friend. And why shouldn't he do Art, if he wants to? You think you're so clever. Miss Ziggle's pet! And Dogbert's a lot more fun than your stupid iguana will ever be!'

'Alex! I only . . .'

'Forget it, Rob. Go and find some girl. The world is full of them.'

I march away, feeling magnificent (and a little shaky). By the time I catch up with Mark, who has finally caught up with Dogbert, we are all out of breath, and we collapse on a grass verge, puffing and panting.

'I'm sorry, Mark! Rob's stupid. I hate him.' (He insulted Dogbert! Dogbert is a *special* dog . . .)

'Why were you with him, then?'

'I didn't want to be. I want to be with you . . .'

(Our eyes meet. The music swells, etc. etc. ETC . . . At least we've now gone beyond the Incredibly Polite stage . . .)

Sunday November 5th

It is Dogbert's least favourite night of the entire year – Bonfire Night! He is safely locked away in his house, with his paws over his ears.

Being boring and normal (this is debatable) my family has decided to have their fireworks on the same night as everyone else. I have invited Mark, Abby and James to join us. It is like old times! Only better.

Mum cooks sausages and baked beans. I tell her off about the baked beans, since I am increasingly worried about damage to the ozone layer. In my opinion, the manufacturers of baked beans are totally irresponsible. When I leave school, I intend to campaign for baked beans to be made illegal.

'Cows do a lot more damage,' says Dad, 'to the ozone layer. And they eat grass.'

One of my brothers suggests feeding cows on baked beans.

I despair of my family, although there is something reassuring about their utter hopelessness. I know they are there for me, and I don't have to pretend to be anything other than myself. I have come to the conclusion that Rob and his family put on an act the whole time (his mum looks like something straight out of pantomime!). They probably think they are funny and clever, but I think it must get boring if you have to live with it all the time. Rob would die if he knew that I now think he is BORING! I was taken in by his act to begin with, but I now see through it. I doubt whether he has many real friends – male or female. I think I feel sorry for him. I appreciate my own family more, and the fact that I have real friends.

Thursday November 9th

The trials and tribulations of 'normal' family life! I may have mentioned the silly, trilly voice which Mum puts on whenever a boy calls at our house to see me (this happens all the time, of course, since I am so irresistible, ha ha). Almost worse than Mum's silly voice is the way my big sister Daisy is inclined to greet any boy who calls.

'What do YOU want?' This is her characteristic friendly (NOT) greeting. She seems intent on scaring away any boy who takes an interest in me, and I am NOT happy about this. The last time she opened the door to Mark (and she frequently gets to the door first,

WHAT DO YOU WANT??!

FLOWER POWER SHOWER CAP

even though I do my best to barge her out of the way), she was wearing a Madagascan mud facial mask and a floral print shower cap (a flower power shower cap! Except that we don't have a power shower, just a sort of hose thing which keeps falling off the tap). I felt sorry for Mark, being confronted by the Sister from Hell. I try to excuse her appearance and attitude by explaining that she is mad. But I don't want any boy to draw the wrong conclusion (or it may be the right one) that madness runs in our family. (Compared to Rob and his family I would say that we are relatively sane and normal.)

I am aware that Daisy has a protective Big Sister attitude towards me (particularly since the Kevin Incident, which was mentioned in my last diary), but I don't want her protection (unless I specifically ask for it). All I want is to borrow her new advanced Ultra Sultry Luscious Lash mascara, which she is too mean to let me use.

I have to admire Diggory for seeing through the Madagascan mud facial mask to the beautiful person within (I am sure there is one – she can be nice). But she gives him a hard time, and is inclined to say things like 'What, NOW?' to the poor chap. I'm sure I heard him say 'Yes, dear,' the other day. Cringe. Perhaps he was being sarcastic. I don't think so. It is not in Diggory's nature to be sarcastic.

Other people's relationships are certainly baffling. I find relationships within my own family confusing enough. Mum keeps saying to me: 'You will talk to me, Alex, won't you? If there's a problem.' I reply: 'Yes. But I'm fine. Really.' Then it occurs to me that I have plenty of problems, and perhaps I ought to choose one (Select-A-Problem) and talk to her about it. Maybe she feels shut out because I choose not to discuss every detail of my life with her. It would be nice to have a close mother-daughter relationship such as Abby seems to have with her mum. Sometimes I feel envious. There is only one of Abby (just as well) so she has her mother's undivided attention whereas my own mum is torn in six different directions, or seven if you include Dad. I imagine myself with my arm round Mum, leaning my head on her shoulder and saying things like: 'My mum's my best friend. She's great.' Feeling quite misty-eyed, I find Mum and say: 'Mum? Can I talk to you?'

'Not now, Alex. I'm in the airing cupboard. Could you feed the cat?'

Oh well. I tried. But it seems that I have a mother who puts the airing cupboard and the cat before her own daughter. (**Note:** It is still somehow reassuring to find Mum in the airing cupboard. At least I know where she is. If I had a mother like Rob's, she would be far too busy doing clever things, saying clever things and meeting other clever people to have any time for me. I cannot imagine talking to Rob's mum about boyfriend problems. She would laugh at me and make me feel stupid. Mum never does this.)

Friday November 10th

My poem has been published in the school magazine (CRINGE!). Beside it I have drawn Mark's face, looking sad, and my face, looking sorry (although I look more like a dying duck – a Llandafdaffy one), and I have framed the two faces in a heart shape, with a small crack in it dripping blood/tears (I am not sure which).

'That's really sweet, Alex!' says Rob, who is reading the school magazine, just to embarrass me. (Hmm. Is he sending me up? He's a funny chap. Perhaps he feels sorry for upsetting me. But I'm not interested.)

Mr Chubb asks me to autograph his copy of the

MY DRAWING FOR THE
SCHOOL MAGAZINE

school magazine. Mr Chubb is mad. He does not even have pregnancy hormones as an excuse (Mr Chubb is definitely NOT pregnant, just a little overweight).

It is a relief to get home.

Wednesday November 15th

Parents' evening at St Rhubarb's. Mum and Dad are upstairs getting ready. I know what Mum is going to wear – the dreadful fucshia-pink suit which she NEVER wears on any other occasion (at all other times she has good taste in clothes for someone of her age).

Dad has announced that he intends to go to this parents' evening because he wishes to have 'a few words' with Miss Ziggle. (He hasn't met her before, but he is still upset about my drawing of *The Kiss*, and he is also not satisfied that my talent is being given sufficient encouragement – which is mega-EMBARRASSING, and I wish he would decide not to go after all. No such luck.)

When Dad comes downstairs, he is wearing – I DON'T BELIEVE IT – his old school tie (no, oh no – please god, NO!) AND an ancient striped blazer which he has discovered in the spiders' web-covered depths of his wardrobe. It is a bit tight on him . . .

Cringing horribly, I follow Mum and Dad at a distance (perhaps people will assume that we are not related) into the brightly lit school hall.

'So where's Miss Ziggle?' Dad demands, in a no-nonsense, uncompromising tone of voice.

'May I help you?' Miss Ziggle gives Dad a dazzling smile and shakes him warmly by the hand. 'You must be Alex's father. I can see the family likeness.'

(Surely NOT.)

Dad seems to have lost the power of speech. He stands there, holding Miss Ziggle's hand, like a man who has fallen under some kind of spell. Mum clears her throat in a certain way which brings Dad immediately to his senses.

'Shall we sit down?' Miss Ziggle asks. (Dad needs to.) I decide to leave them to it, and wander away to look at the picture displays which decorate the walls of the hall. Most of the paintings seem to be Rob's. There are a few of mine. Strangely, Mark's painting of

'Rejection' is up there, too.

Rob's mum is at the parents' evening, wearing an even bigger turban, and booming at all the teachers about the importance of Art (it doesn't matter whether they are History/Geography/Maths teachers – she is only there to boom at them about Art). Mr Hargreaves, the headteacher, is ushering her around, bowing and scraping (I think he is hoping for some sort of donation from the Potsworthy Foundation – who own the Potsworthy Collection, etc. etc.).

I find Mark, and we agree that our parents are embarrassing but not as embarrassing as Rob's mum (or his dad, who is not at the parents' evening – too busy farting on stage).

I am reminded once again that, after my experience with Rob's family, I am thankful that I have *normal* parents. (At this moment Dad walks past wearing his old school tie and ill-fitting blazer, and suddenly I am not so sure . . . I am relieved to get home.)

Thursday November 16th
It is a relief to get to school. Dad has not stopped raving about Miss Ziggle since we left the parents' evening last night. I don't know how Mum puts up with it. I have been told about forty times how lucky I am to have such a good teacher (for 'good', read 'dazzling smile, lovely figure', etc.).

Dad also told me that Miss Ziggle's name is Zelda (did I really want to know this? Zelda Ziggle . . .). I despair of parents and teachers alike.

Monday November 20th
There is mounting excitement about the prize giving, which is scheduled for Friday. Who will the mystery celebrity be? Everyone's working hard in the hope that they'll win a prize and get to shake the celebrity's hand.

'You're all mad,' says Rob. 'It'll turn out to be some boring old person who isn't really famous at all. You'll see.'

A few people agree with him (and I have a sneaking suspicion he may be right . . .).

Friday November 24th
The school hall is packed with parents, teachers and the rest of the school who have all gathered for the Year

Eleven Prize Giving. There is an air of hushed excitement and expectation. The identity of the mystery celebrity is about to be revealed!

Everyone falls silent as Mr Hargreaves, the headteacher, stands up to speak. 'Welcome to the Year Eleven Prize Giving. I would like to extend a special welcome to our guest speaker, who has kindly accepted our invitation to be here today to present the prizes. Ladies, gentlemen and Rhubarbians, would you please put your hands together and welcome . . .' (WHO? WHO IS IT GOING TO BE??!) '. . . Arnold Smoothgrass, who is well-known to us all as the presenter of the television programme "Gardening For

ARNOLD SMOOTHGRASS

All". Ladies and gentlemen, I give you – ARNOLD SMOOTHGRASS!!!'

There is a polite but not excessive burst of applause. Clare's mum gives a shriek and has to be restrained by her husband (she is in lurve with Arnold Smoothgrass – poor woman). The whole of Year Eleven shrink down in our seats, hoping desperately that we are not going to win any prizes. We all bitterly regret working hard.

Arnold Smoothgrass is wearing one of the hand-knitted colourful sweaters for which he is well-known. His thick black hair is combed straight across his head, with a neat side parting. NIGHTMARE!

The first poor victim to win a prize is a quiet girl called Angela who wins the Theobold Throstlethwaite Award for Advanced Thwotting (or something like that – it is a prize for making a Good Effort, anyway). Angela blushes bright red and looks as though she is going to cry, as a photographer from the *Rhubarb Evening Record* makes her pause in mid-handshake with Mr Smoothgrass so that he can preserve the moment for ALL TIME. (Angela's parents will later buy the photo from the *Rhubarb Evening Record*, have it enlarged, frame it, display it on the mantelpiece, and the poor girl will never live it down. She will be in therapy for the next five years . . .)

I am dismayed when it is announced that I am the winner of the Jolly Poetry Prize. Mrs Jolly is evidently feeling much better now, because she is standing up on stage beside Arnold Smoothgrass without being instantly sick. I creep up on to the stage, trying to be invisible (I am the poet known as Anon). Shaking Arnold Smoothgrass's hand is like shaking a kipper – limp and clammy (this man has never wielded a spade in his life!).

Rowena wins the Sports Prize. When she shakes Mr Smoothgrass's hand, I notice him wince with pain. He is noticeably subdued after this encounter.

Rob wins the Art Prize (surPRIZE surPRIZE! Ha ha). When he goes to collect his award, he greets Arnold Smoothgrass like an old friend: 'Hi, Arnie! It's good to see you again!' Arnold grins nervously (I think he is beginning to regret coming to St Rhubarb's . . .).

Various other prizes are awarded (most of them to Rob – the school *definitely* wants a donation from the Potsworthy Foundation . . .), and then Arnold Smoothgrass drones on for about half an hour about gardening and his career in television, until most of us are nearly asleep (apart from Clare's mum, who is hanging on his every word . . .).

Later

Mum insists on displaying my small trophy on the mantelpiece (the Jolly Poetry Prize).

'They've engraved your name on it, dear!'

'Yes.'

'I still think you should have won the Art Prize,' Dad

grumbles. 'Instead of that strange chap with the green hair. I think I'd better write to the school.'

'Yes, Dad.'

Thursday December 1st

Christmas is coming! The geese are going on a strict diet (if they have any sense). Mum is getting flustered. She keeps trying to hide parcels (and herself) from my brothers and Rosie, and they keep discovering the parcels (and Mum). Mum and Dad ask me nearly every day what I would like for Christmas, and when I tell them, I get one or more of the following predictable answers:

1) No.

2) NO.

3) What's that? What IS it? You can't have it anyway.

4) That's too expensive.

5) I wasn't allowed one of those at your age. (They weren't invented.)

6) Think of something sensible and . . . er . . . useful. Aunty Pat wants to know what you'd like.

YES, YOU <u>WILL</u> HAVE A CHRISTMAS STOCKING...

7) You can't ask Aunty Pat for THAT! Honestly, Alex.

8) OK. I'll give you money. Not too much. There are lots of other people to consider.

9) Yes, I realise you'd like something to unwrap as well.

10) How about a nice surprise?

11) Yes, you WILL be having a stocking. Same as usual.

Friday December 9th

Early evening

Carol singing with Diggory and Daisy and their friends and colleagues from the library and garden centre. I was persuaded to join them as they are collecting for charity, but it turns out to be a seriously embarrassing experience. Diggory's singing voice is incredibly loud (for a librarian) and drowns everyone else's, which wouldn't be so bad if he was singing in tune. But he sounds like a lovesick cat, and I keep expecting an upstairs window to open in one of the houses and someone to throw a bucket of water over us. I am sent to knock on people's doors with the collecting box, and I suspect that most people are paying us to go away, as they shut their doors again quickly after dropping a few coins in the box.

We visit Clare's house and her parents (who must be tone deaf) give us a round of applause, and ask us to repeat 'Hark the Herald Angels Sing'. Clare's dad stands on his doorstep, conducting (groan – the things I do for charity!).

Saturday December 10th

We are at Tracey's house, discussing what we want for Christmas.

'I want a snood,' says Clare.

'A what?'

'A snood?'

'What's that?'

'A sort of hood thing. It covers your whole head. It's really warm.'

'Try a paper bag,' Tracey suggests. 'It's cheaper.'

Clare ignores her and continues: 'Oh, and I want all six volumes of poetry by Andrew Static.' (I know that Christmas should be a time of peace, joy and hope, but I begin to think there is no hope for Clare.)

'You'll be snood under!' remarks Tracey, wittily. 'But you can keep your silly old snood. I'm just asking for money so I can go to all the New Year sales and buy loads of stuff.'

'Me, too. That's what I'm having.'

'What? Money?'

'Yes. And stuff.'

'That's what Christmas is about, isn't it? Stuff. The shops are full of stuff. People wrap up stuff and give it to each other.'

CLARE IN A SNOOD (DIFFERENT FROM BEING IN A MOOD...)

'Do you still get a stocking?'

HO HO HO!

'Er . . .'

'So do I! Let's read our Christmas horoscopes.'

Mystic Marge predicts that I will meet a short, fat stranger with a white beard, and wearing a red suit. No doubt this is Mystic Marge's idea of A JOKE. Funny.

Later on we go Christmas shopping. I decide (in a fit of generosity and goodwill) to buy my whole family a computer game (it happens to be one which I have been longing to have a go on). I buy some recycled cards to give to all my friends. There are decorations everywhere and crowds of shoppers, and Christmas music blaring out. I get a lump in my throat (I shouldn't have eaten those roast turkey and stuffing flavour crisps that Rowena gave me). To stop myself getting too sentimental, I complain to Abby about the monstrous waste of the earth's natural resources involved in Christmas packaging, etc. She tells me to chill out. This is not difficult, since the temperature has dropped and the air feels icy. But I am not dreaming of a white Christmas (I believe in racial equality).

'Tis the season to be jolly tired. I am relieved to get away from the crowds and relax in my room, listening to Ronan O'Hoolahan's Christmas hit, a beautiful song called 'Remember – My Love is For Ever, Not Just for Christmas'.

Monday December 12th

It is the season of goodwill to all men, even little brothers. Unfortunately (for them) my goodwill has now deserted me. Just as we were leaving for school Daniel offered me a sweet. Pleasantly surprised by this unusual display of generosity, I accepted and put the sweet in my mouth. My suspicions have now been raised by the evil sniggering behind my back on the way to school. I should have known. It is a trick sweet which has stained my tongue and my teeth black. There is no time to brush my teeth, even if I happened to have a toothbrush with me. (If I was Clare, I would have a toothbrush with me at all times.) All I can do is glare at my brothers while keeping my mouth firmly shut. They run off, laughing.

To make matters worse, Mark is in a chatty mood, and asks me whether I would like to go to a film with him. All I can do is make a sort of 'mmm mmmmm' noise without moving my lips. I don't want to keep nodding my head because too much nodding of the head is uncool. Mark loses patience.

'Oh well, if you can't be bothered to talk to me, we'd better just forget it.' He marches off in a huff.

I rush to the nearest basin and rinse my mouth out a hundred times. I manage to catch up with Mark.

'Mark! Mark! I lost my voice, that's all! But I've found it again. And I'd really like to go to the film!'

'Oh, er . . . good! Have you been eating liquorice?'

Later that night I put itching powder in my brothers' beds. (I have visited the shop where they buy their horrid jokes.)

Tuesday December 13th

Dad is in a foul mood after the Christmas tree fell on him while he was sitting in his chair reading the newspaper.

(In a funny sort of way it is comforting to see him there in his familiar armchair, wearing his sad old slippers and cardigan, although not necessarily buried by a tree. I couldn't bear to have a dad like Rob's. I could never relax if I thought my dad was going to appear in front of my friends wearing pink boxer shorts – or if he lived in a caravan in the garden and hardly spoke to Mum . . .)

Our Christmas tree this year is big and Dad had put it in a Christmas-tree stand, which seemed like a good idea at the time, until the cat decides to climb the tree, makes it nearly to the top (I think it wants to kill and eat the fairy), at which point one of my brothers shouts 'TIMBER!' and Dad disappears under a shower of green needles, tinsel, coloured balls, fairy lights and panicking cat. He emerges looking as if he is undergoing an acupuncture treatment involving the use of many small green needles.

'Never mind, dear,' says Mum, mildly. 'At least the

THE CAT WANTS TO KILL AND
EAT THE FAIRY...

ACUPUNCTURE INVOLVING THE USE OF MANY SMALL GREEN NEEDLES . . .

tree lights worked first time.' At this point the tree lights all go out, and so does every single light in the house and we are plunged into total eclipse-like darkness.

'Oh dear.'

Yes. It's Christmas. Fa la la, etc.

Mum lights some candles, and it is all very romantic, although Dad's language as he stumbles off to the fuse box is decidedly NOT romantic. (From what he is saying, it sounds as if some of the pine needles have worked their way into his underpants – not a good thought. The spirit of Christmas seems to have deserted him, and he is having uncharitable thoughts towards the cat, the tree, etc. But this is all very NORMAL.)

Friday December 19th

(I have pressed the fast-forward button on my diary . . . I can't wait for Christmas! I'm like a big kid, and I still get a stocking – EMBARRASSING. But fun. The only thing about Christmas which I don't approve of is the mass slaughter of turkeys, which seems totally un-necessary. I won't eat the stuff. But I like the stuffing.)

HO HO HO!

MR CHUBB IS DRESSED UP
AS FATHER CHRISTMAS

This evening it is the St Rhubarb's end-of-term Christmas disco. Mr Chubb is dressed up as Father Christmas and is full of good cheer.

'Ho ho ho! What do you want for Christmas, Alex?'

'Er. World peace, Mr Chubb.'

'Ho ho ho! Right. Yes . . . have a good evening!'

I escape before Mr Chubb can ask me to dance (he has a nasty habit of doing this, and I am worried that dancing with Mr Chubb is about as UNCOOL as you can possibly get – unless you are Mrs Chubb).

Fortunately, Mark asks me to dance (this IS cool).

I notice that Rob is surrounded by a group of girls all competing for his attention. I am relieved that I am not one of them. Rob keeps looking at me (probably because I am being so cool, and not chasing after him any more).

When Mark has gone to get some drinks (non-alcoholic Christmas punch, brewed by Mr Chubb and Mrs Jolly), Rob comes over and asks me to dance. I say 'No.' (NO! I said NO!!!) Now I feel SUPERCOOL. Abby is awestruck by my incredible coolness.

But I am happy to be back with Mark, and we dance the rest of the night away together (a slight exaggeration – St Rhubarb's throws us all out at ten thirty p.m.).

Though as we are leaving, I can't help noticing a dishy boy called Tom . . . and he looks at me . . . oh-oh!

LIFE IS SOOOOOOOOOO COMPLICATED!!!!

LIFE IS SOOOOOOOO COMPLICATED...!!!

Sunday 8.00 p.m.   Walking home, I said, "I don't think he's that keen on her. What sort of kiss do you think it was? Was there actual lip contact? Or was it lip to cheek, or lip to corner of mouth?"

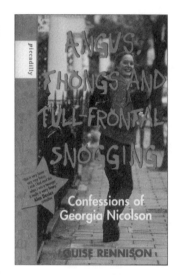

"I think it was lip to corner of mouth, but maybe it was lip to cheek?"

"It wasn't **full-frontal snogging** though, was it?"

"No."

"I think she went for full-frontal and he converted it into lip to corner of mouth . . ."

Saturday 6.58 p.m.
Lindsay was wearing a thong! I don't understand **thongs** – what is the point of them? They just go up your bum, as far as I can tell!

Wednesday 10.30 p.m.
Mrs Next Door complained that **Angus** has been frightening their poodle again. He stalks it. I explained, "Well, he's a Scottish wildcat, that's what they do. They stalk their prey. I have tried to train him but he ate his lead."

*"This is very funny – very, very funny. I wish I had read this when I was a teenager, it really is **very funny**."* Alan Davies

Also available from Piccadilly Press, by
JONATHAN MERES

When Mr. 'hey, call me Dave' Sissons suggests that 5B keep a diary for a whole year, reactions are decidedly mixed! *Yo! Diary!* grants us exclusive access to all areas of six very different fifteen-year-old minds:

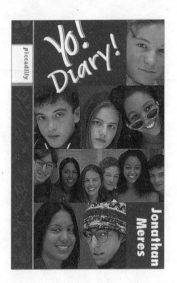

Seb – the rebel and 'Spokesdood for a generation';
Meera – a girl obsessed with astrology;
Steven Stevens – so good his parents named him twice;
Clare – the local neighbourhood Eco Warrior;
Mandy – Ms Personality and Karaoke Queen, and
Craig – convinced that he's the only virgin on the entire planet.

Jonathan Meres has written a riveting and hilarious tale of teenagers teetering on the edge of the millennium! It's a story of changes, drama, love, intrigue and plenty of good old angst! And that's just in the first week!

"Meres' strong, irreverent characterisation and sharp humour (he was a stand-up comedian with his own radio show) make this a book that will achieve an effortless following."
Publishing News

Who'd have thought that Chloë – cool, rich and so sophisticated – would have anything in common with Sinead, who longs for popularity?

And who'd have suspected the problems lurking beneath Jasmin's sparkling smile? And if we're talking about mysteries, then just who is Nick – the fit, supercool guy, but what is he hiding?

And what of Sanjay, who finds his computer so much more user-friendly than people? As five very different teenagers struggle to cope with their changing lives they fall into a friendship which surprises them all . . .

". . . five teenagers from very different backgrounds, the fun and drama of their lives is drawn with humour and sensitivity." Pick of the Paperbacks – The Bookseller

If you would like more information about
books available from Piccadilly Press and how
to order them, please contact us at:

Piccadilly Press Ltd.
5 Castle Road
London
NW1 8PR

Tel: 020 7267 4492
Fax: 020 7267 4493